THE ROMANTIC ADVENTURE
Thomas Hardy

CHAPTER I.

IT was half-past four o'clock (by the testimony of the land-surveyor, my authority for the particulars of this story, a gentleman with the faintest curve of humour on his lips); it was half-past four o'clock on a May morning in the eighteen forties. A dense white fog hung over the Valley of the Exe, ending against the hills on either side.

But though nothing in the vale could be seen from higher ground, notes of differing kinds gave pretty clear indications that bustling life was going on there. This audible presence and visual absence of an active scene had a peculiar effect above the fog level. Nature had laid a white hand over the creatures ensconced within the vale, as a hand might be laid over a nest of chirping birds.

The noises that ascended through the pallid coverlid were perturbed lowings, mingled with human voices in sharps and flats, and the bark of a dog. These, followed by the slamming of a gate, explained as well as eyesight could have done, to any inhabitant of the district, that Dairyman Tucker's under-milker was driving the cows from the meads into the stalls. When a rougher accent joined in the vociferations of man and beast, it would have been realized that the dairy-farmer himself had come out to meet the cows, pail in hand, and white pinafore on; and when, moreover, some women's voices joined in the chorus, that the cows were stalled and proceedings about to commence.

A hush followed, the atmosphere being so stagnant that the milk could be heard buzzing into the pails, together with occasional words of the milkmaids and men.

'Don't ye bide about long upon the road, Margery. You can be back again by skimming-time.'

The rough voice of Dairyman Tucker was the vehicle of this remark. The barton-gate slammed again, and in two or three minutes a something became visible, rising out of the fog in that quarter.

The shape revealed itself as that of a woman having a young and agile gait. The colours and other details of her dress were then disclosed—a bright pink cotton frock (because winter was over); a small woollen shawl of shepherd's plaid (because summer was not come); a white handkerchief tied over her head-gear, because it was so foggy, so damp, and so early; and a straw bonnet and ribbons peeping from under the handkerchief, because it was likely to be a sunny May day.

Her face was of the hereditary type among families down in these parts: sweet in expression, perfect in hue, and somewhat irregular in feature. Her eyes were of a liquid brown. On her arm she carried a withy basket, in which lay several butter-rolls in a nest of wet cabbage-leaves. She was the 'Margery' who had been told not to 'bide about long upon the road.'

She went on her way across the fields, sometimes above the fog, sometimes below it, not much perplexed by its presence except when the track was so indefinite that it ceased to be a guide to the next stile. The dampness was such that innumerable earthworms lay in couples across the path till, startled even by her light tread, they withdrew suddenly into their holes. She kept clear of all trees. Why was that? There was no danger of lightning on such a morning as this. But though the roads were dry the fog had gathered in the boughs, causing them to set up such a dripping as would go clean through the protecting handkerchief like bullets, and spoil the ribbons beneath. The beech and ash were particularly shunned, for they dripped more maliciously than any. It was an instance of woman' s keen appreciativeness of nature' s moods and peculiarities: a man crossing those fields might hardly have perceived that the trees dripped at all.

In less than an hour she had traversed a distance of four miles, and arrived at a latticed cottage in a secluded spot. An elderly woman, scarce awake, answered her knocking. Margery delivered up the butter, and said, 'How is granny this morning? I can' t stay to go up to her, but tell her I have returned what we owed her.'

Her grandmother was no worse than usual: and receiving back the empty basket the girl proceeded to carry out some intention which had not been included in her orders. Instead of returning to the light labours of skimming-time, she hastened on, her direction being towards a little neighbouring town. Before, however, Margery had proceeded far, she met the postman, laden to the neck with letter-bags, of which he had not yet deposited one.

'Are the shops open yet, Samuel?' she said.

'O no,' replied that stooping pedestrian, not waiting to stand upright.

'They won' t be open yet this hour, except the saddler and ironmonger and little tacker-haired machine-man for the farm folk. They downs their shutters at half-past six, then the baker' s at half-past seven, then the draper' s at eight.'

'O, the draper' s at eight.' It was plain that Margery had wanted the draper' s.

The postman turned up a side-path, and the young girl, as though deciding within herself that if she could not go shopping at once she might as well get back for the skimming, retraced her steps.

The public road home from this point was easy but devious. By far the nearest way was by getting over a fence, and crossing the private grounds of a picturesque old country-house, whose chimneys were just visible through the trees. As the house had been shut up for many months, the girl decided to take the straight cut. She pushed her way through the laurel bushes, sheltering her bonnet with the shawl as an additional safeguard, scrambled over an inner boundary, went along through more shrubberies, and stood ready to emerge upon the open lawn. Before doing so she looked around in the wary manner of a poacher. It was not the first time that she had broken fence in her life; but somehow, and all of a sudden, she had felt herself too near womanhood to indulge in such practices with freedom. However, she moved forth, and the house-front stared her in the face, at this higher level unobscured by fog.

It was a building of the medium size, and unpretending, the façade being of stone; and of the Italian elevation made familiar by Inigo Jones and his school. There was a doorway to the lawn, standing at the head of a flight of steps. The shutters of the house were closed, and the blinds of the bedrooms drawn down. Her perception of the fact that no crusty caretaker could see her from the windows led her at once to slacken her pace, and stroll through the flower-beds coolly. A house unblinded is a possible spy, and must be treated accordingly; a house with the shutters together is an insensate heap of stone and mortar, to be faced with indifference.

On the other side of the house the greensward rose to an eminence, whereon stood one of those curious summer shelters sometimes erected on exposed points of view, called an all-the-year-round. In the present case it consisted of four walls radiating from a centre like the arms of a turnstile, with seats in each angle, so that whencesoever the wind came, it was always possible to find a screened corner from which to observe the landscape.

The milkmaid's trackless course led her up the hill and past this erection. At ease as to being watched and scolded as an intruder, her mind flew to other matters; till, at the moment when she was not a yard from the shelter, she heard a foot or feet scraping on the gravel behind it. Some one was in the all-the-year-round, apparently occupying the seat on the other side; as was proved when, on turning, she saw an elbow, a man's elbow, projecting over the edge.

Now the young woman did not much like the idea of going down the hill under the eyes of this person, which she would have to do if she went on, for as an intruder she was liable to be called back and questioned upon her business there. Accordingly she crept softly up and sat in the seat behind, intending to remain there until her companion should leave.

4

This he by no means seemed in a hurry to do. What could possibly have brought him there, what could detain him there, at six o' clock on a morning of mist when there was nothing to be seen or enjoyed of the vale beneath, puzzled her not a little. But he remained quite still, and Margery grew impatient. She discerned the track of his feet in the dewy grass, forming a line from the house steps, which announced that he was an inhabitant and not a chance passer-by. At last she peeped round.

CHAPTER II.

A fine-framed dark-mustachioed gentleman, in dressing-gown and slippers, was sitting there in the damp without a hat on. With one hand he was tightly grasping his forehead, the other hung over his knee. The attitude bespoke with sufficient clearness a mental condition of anguish. He was quite a different being from any of the men to whom her eyes were accustomed. She had never seen mustachios before, for they were not worn by civilians in Lower Wessex at this date. His hands and his face were white—to her view deadly white—and he heeded nothing outside his own existence. There he remained as motionless as the bushes around him; indeed, he scarcely seemed to breathe.

Having imprudently advanced thus far, Margery' s wish was to get back again in the same unseen manner; but in moving her foot for the purpose it grated on the gravel. He started up with an air of bewilderment, and slipped something into the pocket of his dressing-gown. She was almost certain that it was a pistol. The pair stood looking blankly at each other.

'My Gott, who are you?' he asked sternly, and with not altogether an English articulation. 'What do you do here?'

Margery had already begun to be frightened at her boldness in invading the lawn and pleasure-seat. The house had a master, and she had not known of it. 'My name is Margaret Tucker, sir,' she said meekly.

'My father is Dairyman Tucker. We live at Silverthorn Dairy-house.'

'What were you doing here at this hour of the morning?'

She told him, even to the fact that she had climbed over the fence.

'And what made you peep round at me?'

'I saw your elbow, sir; and I wondered what you were doing?'

'And what was I doing?'

'Nothing. You had one hand on your forehead and the other on your knee. I do hope you are not ill, sir, or in deep trouble?' Margery had sufficient tact to say nothing about the pistol.

'What difference would it make to you if I were ill or in trouble? You don' t know me.'

She returned no answer, feeling that she might have taken a liberty in expressing sympathy. But, looking furtively up at him, she discerned to her surprise that he seemed affected by her humane wish, simply as it had been expressed. She had scarcely conceived that such a tall dark man could know what gentle feelings were.

'Well, I am much obliged to you for caring how I am,' said he with a faint smile and an affected lightness of manner which, even to her, only rendered more apparent the gloom beneath. 'I have not slept this past night. I suffer from sleeplessness. Probably you do not.'

Margery laughed a little, and he glanced with interest at the comely picture she presented; her fresh face, brown hair, candid eyes, unpractised manner, country dress, pink hands, empty wicker-basket, and the handkerchief over her bonnet.

'Well,' he said, after his scrutiny, 'I need hardly have asked such a question of one who is Nature's own image . . . Ah, but my good little friend,' he added, recurring to his bitter tone and sitting wearily down,

'you don't know what great clouds can hang over some people's lives, and what cowards some men are in face of them. To escape themselves they travel, take picturesque houses, and engage in country sports. But here it is so dreary, and the fog was horrible this morning!'

'Why, this is only the pride of the morning!' said Margery. 'By-and-by it will be a beautiful day.'

She was going on her way forthwith; but he detained her—detained her with words, talking on every innocent little subject he could think of. He had an object in keeping her there more serious than his words would imply. It was as if he feared to be left alone.

While they still stood, the misty figure of the postman, whom Margery had left a quarter of an hour earlier to follow his sinuous course, crossed the grounds below them on his way to the house. Signifying to Margery by a wave of his hand that she was to step back out of sight, in the hinder angle of the shelter, the gentleman beckoned to the postman to bring the bag to where he stood. The man did so, and again resumed his journey. The stranger unlocked the bag and threw it on the seat, having taken one letter from within. This he read attentively, and his countenance changed.

The change was almost phantasmagorial, as if the sun had burst through the fog upon that face: it became clear, bright, almost radiant. Yet it was but a change that may take place in the commonest human being, provided his countenance be not too wooden, or his artifice have not grown to second nature. He turned to Margery, who was again edging off, and, seizing her hand, appeared as though he were about to embrace her. Checking his impulse, he said, 'My guardian child—my good friend—you have saved me!'

'What from?' she ventured to ask.

'That you may never know.'

She thought of the weapon, and guessed that the letter he had just received had effected this change in his mood, but made no observation till he went on to say, 'What did you tell me was your name, dear girl?'

She repeated her name.

'Margaret Tucker.' He stooped, and pressed her hand. 'Sit down for a moment—one moment,' he said, pointing to the end of the seat, and taking the extremest further end for himself, not to discompose her. She sat down.

'It is to ask a question,' he went on, 'and there must be confidence between us. You have saved me from an act of madness! What can I do for you?'

'Nothing, sir.'

'Nothing?'

'Father is very well off, and we don' t want anything.'

'But there must be some service I can render, some kindness, some votive offering which I could make, and so imprint on your memory as long as you live that I am not an ungrateful man?'

'Why should you be grateful to me, sir?'

He shook his head. 'Some things are best left unspoken. Now think. What would you like to have best in the world?'

Margery made a pretence of reflecting—then fell to reflecting seriously; but the negative was ultimately as undisturbed as ever: she could not decide on anything she would like best in the world; it was too difficult, too sudden.

'Very well—don' t hurry yourself. Think it over all day. I ride this afternoon. You live—where?'

'Silverthorn Dairy-house.'

'I will ride that way homeward this evening. Do you consider by eight o' clock what little article, what little treat, you would most like of any.'

'I will, sir,' said Margery, now warming up to the idea. 'Where shall I meet you? Or will you call at the house, sir?'

'Ah—no. I should not wish the circumstances known out of which our acquaintance rose. It would be more proper—but no.'

7

Margery, too, seemed rather anxious that he should not call. 'I could come out, sir,' she said. 'My father is odd-tempered, and perhaps—'

It was agreed that she should look over a stile at the top of her father's garden, and that he should ride along a bridle-path outside, to receive her answer. 'Margery,' said the gentleman in conclusion, 'now that you have discovered me under ghastly conditions, are you going to reveal them, and make me an object for the gossip of the curious?'

'No, no, sir!' she replied earnestly. 'Why should I do that?'

'You will never tell?'

'Never, never will I tell what has happened here this morning.'

'Neither to your father, nor to your friends, nor to any one?'

'To no one at all,' she said.

'It is sufficient,' he answered. 'You mean what you say, my dear maiden. Now you want to leave me. Good-bye!'

She descended the hill, walking with some awkwardness; for she felt the stranger's eyes were upon her till the fog had enveloped her from his gaze. She took no notice now of the dripping from the trees; she was lost in thought on other things. Had she saved this handsome, melancholy, sleepless, foreign gentleman who had had a trouble on his mind till the letter came? What had he been going to do? Margery could guess that he had meditated death at his own hand. Strange as the incident had been in itself; to her it had seemed stranger even than it was. Contrasting colours heighten each other by being juxtaposed; it is the same with contrasting lives.

Reaching the opposite side of the park there appeared before her for the third time that little old man, the foot-post. As the turnpike-road ran, the postman's beat was twelve miles a day; six miles out from the town, and six miles back at night. But what with zigzags, devious ways, offsets to country seats, curves to farms, looped courses, and triangles to outlying hamlets, the ground actually covered by him was nearer one-and-twenty miles. Hence it was that Margery, who had come straight, was still abreast of him, despite her long pause.

The weighty sense that she was mixed up in a tragical secret with an unknown and handsome stranger prevented her joining very readily in chat with the postman for some time. But a keen interest in her adventure caused her to respond at once when the bowed man of mails said, 'You hit athwart the grounds of Mount Lodge, Miss Margery, or you wouldn't ha' met me here. Well, somebody hey took the old place at last.'

8

In acknowledging her route Margery brought herself to ask who the new gentleman might be.

'Guide the girl' s heart! What! don' t she know? And yet how should ye—he' s only just a-come.—Well, nominal, he' s a fishing gentleman, come for the summer only. But, more to the subject, he' s a foreign noble that' s lived in England so long as to be without any true country: some of his letters call him Baron, some Squire, so that ' a must be born to something that can' t be earned by elbow-grease and Christian conduct. He was out this morning a-watching the fog. "Postman," ' a said, "good-morning: give me the bag." O, yes, ' a' s a civil genteel nobleman enough.'

'Took the house for fishing, did he?'

'That' s what they say, and as it can be for nothing else I suppose it' s true. But, in final, his health' s not good, ' a b' lieve; he' s been living too rithe. The London smoke got into his wyndpipe, till ' a couldn' t eat. However, I shouldn' t mind having the run of his kitchen.'

'And what is his name?'

'Ah—there you have me! ' Tis a name no man' s tongue can tell, or even woman' s, except by pen-and-ink and good scholarship. It begins with X, and who, without the machinery of a clock in' s inside, can speak that? But here ' tis—from his letters.' The postman with his walking-stick wrote upon the ground,

'BARON VON XANTEN'

CHAPTER III.

The day, as she had prognosticated, turned out fine; for weather-wisdom was imbibed with their milk-sops by the children of the Exe Vale. The impending meeting excited Margery, and she performed her duties in her father' s house with mechanical unconsciousness.

Milking, skimming, cheesemaking were done. Her father was asleep in the settle, the milkmen and maids were gone home to their cottages, and the clock showed a quarter to eight. She dressed herself with care, went to the top of the garden, and looked over the stile. The view was eastward, and a great moon hung before her in a sky which had not a cloud. Nothing was moving except on the minutest scale, and she remained leaning over, the night-hawk sounding his croud from the bough of an isolated tree on the open hill side.

Here Margery waited till the appointed time had passed by three-quarters of an hour; but no Baron came. She had been full of an idea, and her heart sank with disappointment. Then at last the pacing of a horse became audible on the soft path without, leading up from the water-meads, simultaneously with which she beheld the form of the stranger, riding home, as he had said.

The moonlight so flooded her face as to make her very conspicuous in the garden-gap. 'Ah my maiden—what is your name—Margery!' he said. 'How came you here? But of course I remember—we were to meet. And it was to be at eight—*proh pudor!*—I have kept you waiting!'

'It doesn' t matter, sir. I' ve thought of something.'

'Thought of something?'

'Yes, sir. You said this morning that I was to think what I would like best in the world, and I have made up my mind.'

'I did say so—to be sure I did,' he replied, collecting his thoughts.

'I remember to have had good reason for gratitude to you.' He placed his hand to his brow, and in a minute alighted, and came up to her with the bridle in his hand. 'I was to give you a treat or present, and you could not think of one. Now you have done so. Let me hear what it is, and I' ll be as good as my word.'

'To go to the Yeomanry Ball that' s to be given this month.'

'The Yeomanry Ball—Yeomanry Ball?' he murmured, as if, of all requests in the world, this was what he had least expected. 'Where is what you call the Yeomanry Ball?'

'At Exonbury.'

'Have you ever been to it before?'

'No, sir.'

'Or to any ball?'

'No.'

'But did I not say a gift—a present?'

'Or a treat?'

'Ah, yes, or a treat,' he echoed, with the air of one who finds himself in a slight fix. 'But with whom would you propose to go?'

'I don' t know. I have not thought of that yet.'

'You have no friend who could take you, even if I got you an invitation?'

Margery looked at the moon. 'No one who can dance,' she said; adding, with hesitation, 'I was thinking that perhaps—'

'But, my dear Margery,' he said, stopping her, as if he half-divined what her simple dream of a cavalier had been; 'it is very odd that you can think of nothing else than going to a Yeomanry Ball. Think again. You are sure there is nothing else?'

'Quite sure, sir,' she decisively answered. At first nobody would have noticed in that pretty young face any sign of decision; yet it was discoverable. The mouth, though soft, was firm in line; the eyebrows were distinct, and extended near to each other. 'I have thought of it all day,' she continued, sadly. 'Still, sir, if you are sorry you offered me anything, I can let you off.'

'Sorry?—Certainly not, Margery,' be said, rather nettled. 'I' ll show you that whatever hopes I have raised in your breast I am honourable enough to gratify. If it lies in my power,' he added with sudden firmness, 'you *shall* go to the Yeomanry Ball. In what building is it to be held?'

'In the Assembly Rooms.'

'And would you be likely to be recognized there? Do you know many people?'

'Not many, sir. None, I may say. I know nobody who goes to balls.'

'Ah, well; you must go, since you wish it; and if there is no other way of getting over the difficulty of having nobody to take you, I' ll take you myself. Would you like me to do so? I can dance.'

'O, yes, sir; I know that, and I thought you might offer to do it. But would you bring me back again?'

'Of course I' ll bring you back. But, by-the-bye, can *you* dance?'

'Yes.'

'What?'

'Reels, and jigs, and country-dances like the New-Rigged-Ship, and Follow-my-Lover, and Haste-to-the-Wedding, and the College Hornpipe, and the Favourite Quickstep, and Captain White' s dance.'

'A very good list—a very good! but unluckily I fear they don' t dance any of those now. But if you have the instinct we may soon cure your ignorance. Let me see you dance a moment.'

She stood out into the garden-path, the stile being still between them, and seizing a side of her skirt with each hand, performed the movements which are even yet far from uncommon in the dances of the villagers of merry England. But her motions, though graceful, were not precisely those which appear in the figures of a modern ball-room.

'Well, my good friend, it is a very pretty sight,' he said, warming up to the proceedings. 'But you dance too well—you dance all over your person—and that's too thorough a way for the present day. I should say it was exactly how they danced in the time of your poet Chaucer; but as people don't dance like it now, we must consider. First I must inquire more about this ball, and then I must see you again.'

'If it is a great trouble to you, sir, I—'

'O no, no. I will think it over. So far so good.'

The Baron mentioned an evening and an hour when he would be passing that way again; then mounted his horse and rode away.

On the next occasion, which was just when the sun was changing places with the moon as an illuminator of Silverthorn Dairy, she found him at the spot before her, and unencumbered by a horse. The melancholy that had so weighed him down at their first interview, and had been perceptible at their second, had quite disappeared. He pressed her right hand between both his own across the stile.

'My good maiden, Gott bless you!' said he warmly. 'I cannot help thinking of that morning! I was too much over-shadowed at first to take in the whole force of it. You do not know all; but your presence was a miraculous intervention. Now to more cheerful matters. I have a great deal to tell—that is, if your wish about the ball be still the same?'

'O yes, sir—if you don't object.'

'Never think of my objecting. What I have found out is something which simplifies matters amazingly. In addition to your Yeomanry Ball at Exonbury, there is also to be one in the next county about the same time. This ball is not to be held at the Town Hall of the county-town as usual, but at Lord Toneborough's, who is colonel of the regiment, and who, I suppose, wishes to please the yeomen because his brother is going to stand for the county. Now I find I could take you there very well, and the great advantage of that ball over the Yeomanry Ball in this county is, that there you would be absolutely unknown, and I also. But do you prefer your own neighbourhood?'

'O no, sir. It is a ball I long to see—I don't know what it is like; it does not matter where.'

'Good. Then I shall be able to make much more of you there, where there is no possibility of recognition. That being settled, the next thing is the dancing. Now reels and such things do not do. For think of this—there is a new dance at Almack's and everywhere else, over which the world has gone crazy.'

'How dreadful!'

'Ah—but that is a mere expression—gone mad. It is really an ancient Scythian dance; but, such is the power of fashion, that, having once been

12

adopted by Society, this dance has made the tour of the Continent in one season.'

'What is its name, sir?'

'The polka. Young people, who always dance, are ecstatic about it, and old people, who have not danced for years, have begun to dance again, on its account. All share the excitement. It arrived in London only some few months ago—it is now all over the country. Now this is your opportunity, my good Margery. To learn this one dance will be enough. They will dance scarce anything else at that ball. While, to crown all, it is the easiest dance in the world, and as I know it quite well I can practise you in the step. Suppose we try?'

Margery showed some hesitation before crossing the stile: it was a Rubicon in more ways than one. But the curious reverence which was stealing over her for all that this stranger said and did was too much for prudence. She crossed the stile.

Withdrawing with her to a nook where two high hedges met, and where the grass was elastic and dry, he lightly rested his arm on her waist, and practised with her the new step of fascination. Instead of music he whispered numbers, and she, as may be supposed, showed no slight aptness in following his instructions. Thus they moved round together, the moon-shadows from the twigs racing over their forms as they turned. The interview lasted about half an hour. Then he somewhat abruptly handed her over the stile and stood looking at her from the other side.

'Well,' he murmured, 'what has come to pass is strange! My whole business after this will be to recover my right mind!'

Margery always declared that there seemed to be some power in the stranger that was more than human, something magical and compulsory, when he seized her and gently trotted her round. But lingering emotions may have led her memory to play pranks with the scene, and her vivid imagination at that youthful age must be taken into account in believing her. However, there is no doubt that the stranger, whoever he might be, and whatever his powers, taught her the elements of modern dancing at a certain interview by moonlight at the top of her father's garden, as was proved by her possession of knowledge on the subject that could have been acquired in no other way.

His was of the first rank of commanding figures, she was one of the most agile of milkmaids, and to casual view it would have seemed all of a piece with Nature's doings that things should go on thus. But there was another side to the case; and whether the strange gentleman were a wild olive tree, or not, it was questionable if the acquaintance would lead to happiness. 'A fleeting romance and a possible calamity;' thus it might have been summed up by the practical.

Margery was in Paradise; and yet she was not at this date distinctly in love with the stranger. What she felt was something more mysterious, more of the nature of veneration. As he looked at her across the stile she spoke timidly, on a subject which had apparently occupied her long.

'I ought to have a ball-dress, ought I not, sir?'

'Certainly. And you shall have a ball-dress.'

'Really?'

'No doubt of it. I won' t do things by halves for my best friend. I have thought of the ball-dress, and of other things also.'

'And is my dancing good enough?'

'Quite—quite.'   He paused, lapsed into thought, and looked at her.

'Margery,' he said, 'do you trust yourself unreservedly to me?'

'O yes, sir,' she replied brightly;   'if I am not too much trouble: if I am good enough to be seen in your society.'

The Baron laughed in a peculiar way.   'Really, I think you may assume as much as that.—However, to business. The ball is on the twenty-fifth, that is next Thursday week; and the only difficulty about the dress is the size. Suppose you lend me this?'   And he touched her on the shoulder to signify a tight little jacket she wore.

Margery was all obedience. She took it off and handed it to him. The Baron rolled and compressed it with all his force till it was about as large as an apple-dumpling, and put it into his pocket.

'The next thing,' he said, 'is about getting the consent of your friends to your going. Have you thought of this?'

'There is only my father. I can tell him I am invited to a party, and I don' t think he' ll mind. Though I would rather not tell him.'

'But it strikes me that you must inform him something of what you intend. I would strongly advise you to do so.'   He spoke as if rather perplexed as to the probable custom of the English peasantry in such matters, and added, 'However, it is for you to decide. I know nothing of the circumstances. As to getting to the ball, the plan I have arranged is this. The direction to Lord Toneborough' s being the other way from my house, you must meet me at Three-Walks-End—in Chillington Wood, two miles or more from here. You know the place? Good. By meeting there we shall save five or six miles of journey—a consideration, as it is a long way. Now, for the last time: are you still firm in your wish for this particular treat and no other? It is not too late to give it up. Cannot you think of something else—something better—some useful

14

household articles you require?'

Margery's countenance, which before had been beaming with expectation, lost its brightness: her lips became close, and her voice broken. 'You have offered to take me, and now—'

'No, no, no,' he said, patting her cheek. 'We will not think of anything else. You shall go.'

CHAPTER IV.

But whether the Baron, in naming such a distant spot for the rendezvous, was in hope she might fail him, and so relieve him after all of his undertaking, cannot be said; though it might have been strongly suspected from his manner that he had no great zest for the responsibility of escorting her.

But he little knew the firmness of the young woman he had to deal with. She was one of those soft natures whose power of adhesiveness to an acquired idea seems to be one of the special attributes of that softness.

To go to a ball with this mysterious personage of romance was her ardent desire and aim; and none the less in that she trembled with fear and excitement at her position in so aiming. She felt the deepest awe, tenderness, and humility towards the Baron of the strange name; and yet she was prepared to stick to her point.

Thus it was that the afternoon of the eventful day found Margery trudging her way up the slopes from the vale to the place of appointment. She walked to the music of innumerable birds, which increased as she drew away from the open meads towards the groves.

She had overcome all difficulties. After thinking out the question of telling or not telling her father, she had decided that to tell him was to be forbidden to go. Her contrivance therefore was this: to leave home this evening on a visit to her invalid grandmother, who lived not far from the Baron's house; but not to arrive at her grandmother's till breakfast-time next morning. Who would suspect an intercalated experience of twelve hours with the Baron at a ball? That this piece of deception was indefensible she afterwards owned readily enough; but she did not stop to think of it then.

It was sunset within Chillington Wood by the time she reached Three-Walks-End—the converging point of radiating trackways, now floored with a carpet of matted grass, which had never known other scythes than the teeth of rabbits and hares. The twitter overhead had ceased, except from a few braver and larger birds, including the cuckoo, who did not fear night at this pleasant time of year. Nobody seemed to be on the spot when she first drew near, but no sooner did Margery stand at the intersection of the roads than a slight crashing became audible, and her patron appeared. He was so transfigured in dress that she scarcely knew him. Under a light great-coat, which was flung open, instead of his ordinary clothes he wore a suit of thin black cloth, an open waistcoat with a frill all down his shirt-front, a white tie, shining boots, no thicker than a glove, a coat that made him look like a bird, and a hat that seemed as if it would open and shut like an accordion.

'I am dressed for the ball—nothing worse,' he said, drily smiling.

'So will you be soon.'

'Why did you choose this place for our meeting, sir?' she asked, looking around and acquiring confidence.

'Why did I choose it? Well, because in riding past one day I observed a large hollow tree close by here, and it occurred to me when I was last with you that this would be useful for our purpose. Have you told your father?'

'I have not yet told him, sir.'

'That's very bad of you, Margery. How have you arranged it, then?'

She briefly related her plan, on which he made no comment, but, taking her by the hand as if she were a little child, he led her through the undergrowth to a spot where the trees were older, and standing at wider distances. Among them was the tree he had spoken of—an elm; huge, hollow, distorted, and headless, with a rift in its side.

'Now go inside,' he said, 'before it gets any darker. You will find there everything you want. At any rate, if you do not you must do without it. I'll keep watch; and don't be longer than you can help to be.'

'What am I to do, sir?' asked the puzzled maiden.

'Go inside, and you will see. When you are ready wave your handkerchief at that hole.'

She stooped into the opening. The cavity within the tree formed a lofty circular apartment, four or five feet in diameter, to which daylight entered at the top, and also through a round hole about six feet from the ground, marking the spot at which a limb had been amputated in the tree's prime. The decayed wood of cinnamon-brown, forming the inner surface of the tree, and the warm evening glow, reflected in at the top, suffused the cavity with a faint mellow radiance.

But Margery had hardly given herself time to heed these things. Her eye had been caught by objects of quite another quality. A large white oblong paper box lay against the inside of the tree; over it, on a splinter, hung a small oval looking-glass.

Margery seized the idea in a moment. She pressed through the rift into the tree, lifted the cover of the box, and, behold, there was disclosed within a lovely white apparition in a somewhat flattened state. It was the ball-dress.

This marvel of art was, briefly, a sort of heavenly cobweb. It was a gossamer texture of precious manufacture, artistically festooned in a dozen flounces or more.

Margery lifted it, and could hardly refrain from kissing it. Had any one told her before this moment that such a dress could exist, she would have said, 'No; it's impossible!' She drew back, went forward, flushed, laughed, raised her hands. To say that the maker of that dress had been an individual of talent was simply understatement: he was a genius, and she sunned herself in the rays of his creation.

She then remembered that her friend without had told her to make haste, and she spasmodically proceeded to array herself. In removing the dress she found satin slippers, gloves, a handkerchief nearly all lace, a fan, and even flowers for the hair. 'O, how could he think of it!' she said, clasping her hands and almost crying with agitation. 'And the glass— how good of him!'

Everything was so well prepared, that to clothe herself in these garments was a matter of ease. In a quarter of an hour she was ready, even to shoes and gloves. But what led her more than anything else into admiration of the Baron's foresight was the discovery that there were half-a-dozen pairs each of shoes and gloves, of varying sizes, out of which she selected a fit.

Margery glanced at herself in the mirror, or at as much as she could see of herself: the image presented was superb. Then she hastily rolled up her old dress, put it in the box, and thrust the latter on a ledge as high as she could reach. Standing on tiptoe, she waved the handkerchief through the upper aperture, and bent to the rift to go out.

But what a trouble stared her in the face. The dress was so airy, so fantastical, and so extensive, that to get out in her new clothes by the rift which had admitted her in her old ones was an impossibility. She heard the Baron's steps crackling over the dead sticks and leaves.

'O, sir!' she began in despair.

'What—can't you dress yourself?' he inquired from the back of the trunk.

'Yes; but I can't get out of this dreadful tree!'

He came round to the opening, stooped, and looked in. 'It is obvious that you cannot,' he said, taking in her compass at a glance; and adding to himself; 'Charming! who would have thought that clothes could do so much!—Wait a minute, my little maid: I have it!' he said more loudly.

With all his might he kicked at the sides of the rift, and by that means broke away several pieces of the rotten touchwood. But, being thinly armed about the feet, he abandoned that process, and went for a fallen branch which lay near. By using the large end as a lever, he tore away pieces of the wooden shell which enshrouded Margery and all her loveliness, till the aperture was large enough for her to pass without tearing her dress. She breathed her relief: the silly girl had begun to fear that she would not get to the ball after all.

He carefully wrapped round her a cloak he had brought with him: it was hooded, and of a length which covered her to the heels.

'The carriage is waiting down the other path,' he said, and gave her his arm. A short trudge over the soft dry leaves brought them to the place indicated.

There stood the brougham, the horses, the coachman, all as still as if they were growing on the spot, like the trees. Margery's eyes rose with some timidity to the coachman's figure.

'You need not mind him,' said the Baron. 'He is a foreigner, and heeds nothing.'

In the space of a short minute she was handed inside; the Baron buttoned up his overcoat, and surprised her by mounting with the coachman. The carriage moved off silently over the long grass of the vista, the shadows deepening to black as they proceeded. Darker and darker grew the night as they rolled on; the neighbourhood familiar to Margery was soon left behind, and she had not the remotest idea of the direction they were taking. The stars blinked out, the coachman lit his lamps, and they bowled on again.

In the course of an hour and a half they arrived at a small town, where they pulled up at the chief inn, and changed horses; all being done so readily that their advent had plainly been expected. The journey was resumed immediately. Her companion never descended to speak to her; whenever she looked out there he sat upright on his perch, with the mien of a person who had a difficult duty to perform, and who meant to perform it properly at all costs. But Margery could not help feeling a certain dread at her situation—almost, indeed, a wish that she had not come. Once or twice she thought, 'Suppose he is a wicked man, who is taking me off to a foreign country, and will never bring me home again.'

But her characteristic persistence in an original idea sustained her against these misgivings except at odd moments. One incident in particular had given her confidence in her escort: she had seen a tear in his eye when she expressed her sorrow for his troubles. He may have divined that her thoughts would take an uneasy turn, for when they stopped for a moment in ascending a hill he came to the window. 'Are you tired, Margery?' he asked kindly.

'No, sir.'

'Are you afraid?'

'N—no, sir. But it is a long way.'

'We are almost there,' he answered. 'And now, Margery,' he said in a lower tone, 'I must tell you a secret. I have obtained this invitation in a peculiar way. I thought it best for your sake not to come in my own name, and this is how I have managed. A man in this county, for whom I have lately done a service, one whom I can trust, and who is personally as unknown here as you and I, has (privately) transferred his card of invitation to me. So that we go under his name. I explain this that you may not say anything imprudent by accident. Keep your ears open and be cautious.' Having said this the Baron retreated again to his place.

'Then he is a wicked man after all!' she said to herself; 'for he is going under a false name.' But she soon had the temerity not to mind it: wickedness of that sort was the one ingredient required just now to finish him off as a hero in her eyes.

They descended a hill, passed a lodge, then up an avenue; and presently there beamed upon them the light from other carriages, drawn up in a file, which moved on by degrees; and at last they halted before a large arched doorway, round which a group of people stood.

'We are among the latest arrivals, on account of the distance,' said the Baron, reappearing. 'But never mind; there are three hours at least for your enjoyment.'

The steps were promptly flung down, and they alighted. The steam from the flanks of their swarthy steeds, as they seemed to her, ascended to the parapet of the porch, and from their nostrils the hot breath jetted forth like smoke out of volcanoes, attracting the attention of all.

CHAPTER V.

The bewildered Margery was led by the Baron up the steps to the interior of the house, whence the sounds of music and dancing were already proceeding. The tones were strange. At every fourth beat a deep and mighty note throbbed through the air, reaching Margery's soul with all the force of a blow.

'What is that powerful tune, sir—I have never heard anything like it?'

she said.

'The Drum Polka,' answered the Baron. 'The strange dance I spoke of and that we practised—introduced from my country and other parts of the continent.'

Her surprise was not lessened when, at the entrance to the ballroom, she heard the names of her conductor and herself announced as 'Mr. and Miss Brown.'

However, nobody seemed to take any notice of the announcement, the room beyond being in a perfect turmoil of gaiety, and Margery's consternation at sailing under false colours subsided. At the same moment she observed awaiting them a handsome, dark-haired, rather *petite* lady in cream-coloured satin. 'Who is she?' asked Margery of the Baron.

'She is the lady of the mansion,' he whispered. 'She is the wife of a peer of the realm, the daughter of a marquis, has five Christian names; and hardly ever speaks to commoners, except for political purposes.'

'How divine—what joy to be here!' murmured Margery, as she contemplated the diamonds that flashed from the head of her ladyship, who was just inside the ball-room door, in front of a little gilded chair, upon which she sat in the intervals between one arrival and another. She had come down from London at great inconvenience to herself; openly to promote this entertainment.

As Mr. and Miss Brown expressed absolutely no meaning to Lady Toneborough (for there were three Browns already present in this rather mixed assembly), and as there was possibly a slight awkwardness in poor Margery's manner, Lady Toneborough touched their hands lightly with the tips of her long gloves, said, 'How d'ye do,' and turned round for more comers.

'Ah, if she only knew we were a rich Baron and his friend, and not Mr. and Miss Brown at all, she wouldn't receive us like that, would she?' whispered Margery confidentially.

'Indeed, she wouldn't!' drily said the Baron. 'Now let us drop into the dance at once; some of the people here, you see, dance much worse than you.'

Almost before she was aware she had obeyed his mysterious influence, by giving him one hand, placing the other upon his shoulder, and swinging with him round the room to the steps she had learnt on the sward.

At the first gaze the apartment had seemed to her to be floored with black ice; the figures of the dancers appearing upon it upside down. At last she realized that it was highly-polished oak, but she was none the less afraid to move.

'I am afraid of falling down,' she said.

'Lean on me; you will soon get used to it,' he replied. 'You have no nails in your shoes now, dear.'

His words, like all his words to her, were quite true. She found it amazingly easy in a brief space of time. The floor, far from hindering her, was a positive assistance to one of her natural agility and litheness. Moreover, her marvellous dress of twelve flounces inspired her as nothing else could have done. Externally a new creature, she was prompted to new deeds. To feel as well-dressed as the other women around her is to set any woman at her ease, whencesoever she may have come: to feel much better dressed is to add radiance to that ease.

Her prophet's statement on the popularity of the polka at this juncture was amply borne out. It was among the first seasons of its general adoption in country houses; the enthusiasm it excited to-night was beyond description, and scarcely credible to the youth of the present day. A new motive power had been introduced into the world of poesy—the polka, as a counterpoise to the new motive power that had been introduced into the world of prose—steam.

Twenty finished musicians sat in the music gallery at the end, with romantic mop-heads of raven hair, under which their faces and eyes shone like fire under coals.

The nature and object of the ball had led to its being very inclusive. Every rank was there, from the peer to the smallest yeoman, and Margery got on exceedingly well, particularly when the recuperative powers of supper had banished the fatigue of her long drive.

Sometimes she heard people saying, 'Who are they?—brother and sister—father and daughter? And never dancing except with each other—how odd?' But of this she took no notice.

When not dancing the watchful Baron took her through the drawing-rooms and picture-galleries adjoining, which to-night were thrown open like the rest of the house; and there, ensconcing her in some curtained nook, he drew her attention to scrap-books, prints, and albums, and left her to amuse herself with turning them over till the dance in which she was practised should again be called. Margery would much have preferred to roam about during these intervals; but the words of the Baron were law, and as he commanded so she acted. In such alternations the evening winged away; till at last came the gloomy words,

'Margery, our time is up.'

'One more—only one!' she coaxed, for the longer they stayed the more freely and gaily moved the dance. This entreaty he granted; but on her asking for yet another, he was inexorable. 'No,' he said. 'We have a long way to go.'

Then she bade adieu to the wondrous scene, looking over her shoulder as they withdrew from the hall; and in a few minutes she was cloaked and in the carriage. The Baron mounted to his seat on the box, where she saw him light a cigar; they plunged under the trees, and she leant back, and gave herself up to contemplate the images that filled her brain. The natural result followed: she fell asleep.

She did not awake till they stopped to change horses; when she saw against the stars the Baron sitting as erect as ever. 'He watches like the Angel Gabriel, when all the world is asleep!' she thought.

With the resumption of motion she slept again, and knew no more till he touched her hand and said, 'Our journey is done—we are in Chillington Wood.'

It was almost daylight. Margery scarcely knew herself to be awake till she was out of the carriage and standing beside the Baron, who, having told the coachman to drive on to a certain point indicated, turned to her.

'Now,' he said, smiling, 'run across to the hollow tree; you know where it is. I'll wait as before, while you perform the reverse operation to that you did last night.' She took no heed of the path now, nor regarded whether her pretty slippers became scratched by the brambles or no. A walk of a few steps brought her to the particular tree which she had left about nine hours earlier. It was still gloomy at this spot, the morning not being clear.

She entered the trunk, dislodged the box containing her old clothing, pulled off the satin shoes, and gloves, dress, and in ten minutes emerged in the cotton and shawl of shepherd's plaid.

Baron was not far off. 'Now you look the milkmaid again,' he said, coming towards her. 'Where is the finery?'

'Packed in the box, sir, as I found it.' She spoke with more humility now. The difference between them was greater than it had been at the ball.

'Good,' he said. 'I must just dispose of it; and then away we go.'

He went back to the tree, Margery following at a little distance. Bringing forth the box, he pulled out the dress as carelessly as if it had been rags. But this was not all. He gathered a few dry sticks, crushed the lovely garment into a loose billowy heap, threw the gloves, fan, and shoes on the top, then struck a light and ruthlessly set fire to the whole. Margery was agonized. She ran forward; she implored and entreated.

'Please, sir—do spare it—do! My lovely dress—my-dear, dear slippers—my fan—it is cruel! Don' t burn them, please!'

'Nonsense. We shall have no further use for them if we live a hundred years.'

'But spare a bit of it—one little piece, sir—a scrap of the lace—one bow of the ribbon—the lovely fan—just something!'

But he was as immoveable as Rhadamanthus. 'No,' he said, with a stern gaze of his aristocratic eye. 'It is of no use for you to speak like that. The things are my property. I undertook to gratify you in what you might desire because you had saved my life. To go to a ball, you said. You might much more wisely have said anything else, but no; you said, to go to a ball. Very well—I have taken you to a ball. I have brought you back. The clothes were only the means, and I dispose of them my own way. Have I not a right to?'

'Yes, sir,' she said meekly.

He gave the fire a stir, and lace and ribbons, and the twelve flounces, and the embroidery, and all the rest crackled and disappeared. He then put in her hands the butter basket she had brought to take on to her grandmother' s, and accompanied her to the edge of the wood, where it merged in the undulating open country in which her granddame dwelt.

'Now, Margery,' he said, 'here we part. I have performed my contract—at some awkwardness, if I was recognized. But never mind that. How do you feel—sleepy?'

'Not at all, sir,' she said.

'That long nap refreshed you, eh? Now you must make me a promise. That if I require your presence at any time, you will come to me . . . I am a man of more than one mood,' he went on with sudden solemnity;

'and I may have desperate need of you again, to deliver me from that darkness as of Death which sometimes encompasses me. Promise it, Margery—promise it; that, no matter what stands in the way, you will come to me if I require you.'

'I would have if you had not burnt my pretty clothes!' she pouted.

'Ah—ungrateful!'

'Indeed, then, I will promise, sir,' she said from her heart. 'Wherever I am, if I have bodily strength I will come to you.'

He pressed her hand. 'It is a solemn promise,' he replied. 'Now I must go, for you know your way.'

'I shall hardly believe that it has not been all a dream!' she said, with a childish instinct to cry at his withdrawal. 'There will be nothing left of last night—nothing of my dress, nothing of my pleasure, nothing of the place!'

'You shall remember it in this way,' said he. 'We'll cut our initials on this tree as a memorial, so that whenever you walk this path you will see them.'

Then with a knife he inscribed on the smooth bark of a beech tree the letters M.T., and underneath a large X.

'What, have you no Christian name, sir?' she said.

'Yes, but I don't use it. Now, good-bye, my little friend.—What will you do with yourself to-day, when you are gone from me?' he lingered to ask.

'Oh—I shall go to my granny's,' she replied with some gloom;

'and have breakfast, and dinner, and tea with her, I suppose; and in the evening I shall go home to Silverthorn Dairy, and perhaps Jim will come to meet me, and all will be the same as usual.'

'Who is Jim?'

'O, he's nobody—only the young man I've got to marry some day.'

'What!—you engaged to be married?—Why didn't you tell me this before?'

'I—I don't know, sir.'

'What is the young man's name?'

'James Hayward.'

'What is he?'

'A master lime-burner.'

'Engaged to a master lime-burner, and not a word of this to me! Margery, Margery! when shall a straightforward one of your sex be found! Subtle even in your simplicity! What mischief have you caused me to do, through not telling me this? I wouldn't have so endangered anybody's happiness for a thousand pounds. Wicked girl that you were; why didn't you tell me?'

'I thought I'd better not!' said Margery, beginning to be frightened.

'But don't you see and understand that if you are already the property of a young man, and he were to find out this night's excursion, he may be angry with you and part from you for ever? With him already in the field I had no right to take you at all; he undoubtedly ought to have taken you; which really might have been arranged, if you had not deceived me by saying you had nobody.'

Margery's face wore that aspect of woe which comes from the

24

repentant consciousness of having been guilty of an enormity. 'But he wasn't good enough to take me, sir!' she said, almost crying; 'and he isn't absolutely my master until I have married him, is he?'

'That's a subject I cannot go into. However, we must alter our tactics. Instead of advising you, as I did at first, to tell of this experience to your friends, I must now impress on you that it will be best to keep a silent tongue on the matter—perhaps for ever and ever. It may come right some day, and you may be able to say "All's well that ends well." Now, good morning, my friend. Think of Jim, and forget me.'

'Ah, perhaps I can't do that,' she said, with a tear in her eye, and a full throat.

'Well—do your best. I can say no more.'

He turned and retreated into the wood, and Margery, sighing, went on her way.

CHAPTER VI.

Between six and seven o' clock in the evening of the same day a young man descended the hills into the valley of the Exe, at a point about midway between Silverthorn and the residence of Margery's grandmother, four miles to the east.

He was a thoroughbred son of the country, as far removed from what is known as the provincial, as the latter is from the out-and-out gentleman of culture. His trousers and waistcoat were of fustian, almost white, but he wore a jacket of old-fashioned blue West-of-England cloth, so well preserved that evidently the article was relegated to a box whenever its owner engaged in such active occupations as he usually pursued. His complexion was fair, almost florid, and he had scarcely any beard.

A novel attraction about this young man, which a glancing stranger would know nothing of, was a rare and curious freshness of atmosphere that appertained to him, to his clothes, to all his belongings, even to the room in which he had been sitting. It might almost have been said that by adding him and his implements to an over-crowded apartment you made it healthful. This resulted from his trade. He was a lime-burner; he handled lime daily; and in return the lime rendered him an incarnation of salubrity. His hair was dry, fair, and frizzled, the latter possibly by the operation of the same caustic agent. He carried as a walking-stick a green sapling, whose growth had been contorted to a corkscrew pattern by a twining honeysuckle.

As he descended to the level ground of the water-meadows he cast his glance westward, with a frequency that revealed him to be in search of some object in the distance. It was rather difficult to do this, the low sunlight dazzling his eyes by glancing from the river away there, and from the 'carriers' (as they were called) in his path—narrow artificial brooks for conducting the water over the grass. His course was something of a zigzag from the necessity of finding points in these carriers convenient for jumping. Thus peering and leaping and winding, he drew near the Exe, the central river of the miles-long mead.

A moving spot became visible to him in the direction of his scrutiny, mixed up with the rays of the same river. The spot got nearer, and revealed itself to be a slight thing of pink cotton and shepherd's plaid, which pursued a path on the brink of the stream. The young man so shaped his trackless course as to impinge on the path a little ahead of this coloured form, and when he drew near her he smiled and reddened. The girl smiled back to him; but her smile had not the life in it that the young man's had shown.

'My dear Margery—here I am!' he said gladly in an undertone, as with a last leap he crossed the last intervening carrier, and stood at her side.

'You've come all the way from the kiln, on purpose to meet me, and you shouldn't have done it,' she reproachfully returned.

'We finished there at four, so it was no trouble; and if it had been— why, I should ha' come.'

A small sigh was the response.

'What, you are not even so glad to see me as you would be to see your dog or cat?' he continued. 'Come, Mis'ess Margery, this is rather hard. But, by George, how tired you dew look! Why, if you'd been up all night your eyes couldn't be more like tea-saucers. You've walked tew far, that's what it is. The weather is getting warm now, and the air of these low-lying meads is not strengthening in summer. I wish you lived up on higher ground with me, beside the kiln. You'd get as strong as a hoss! Well, there; all that will come in time.'

Instead of saying yes, the fair maid repressed another sigh.

'What, won't it, then?' he said.

'I suppose so,' she answered. 'If it is to be, it is.'

'Well said—very well said, my dear.'

'And if it isn't to be it isn't.'

'What? Who's been putting that into your head? Your grumpy granny, I suppose. However, how is she? Margery, I have been thinking to-day—in fact, I was thinking it yesterday and all the week—that really we might settle our little business this summer.'

26

'This summer?' she repeated, with some dismay. 'But the partnership? Remember it was not to be till after that was completed.'

'There I have you!' said he, taking the liberty to pat her shoulder, and the further liberty of advancing his hand behind it to the other. 'The partnership is settled. ' Tis "Vine and Hayward, lime-burners," now, and "Richard Vine" no longer. Yes, Cousin Richard has settled it so, for a time at least, and ' tis to be painted on the carts this week—blue letters—yaller ground. I' ll boss one of ' em, and drive en round to your door as soon as the paint is dry, to show ' ee how it looks?'

'Oh, I am sure you needn' t take that trouble, Jim; I can see it quite well enough in my mind,' replied the young girl—not without a flitting accent of superiority.

'Hullo,' said Jim, taking her by the shoulders, and looking at her hard.

'What dew that bit of incivility mean? Now, Margery, let' s sit down here, and have this cleared.' He rapped with his stick upon the rail of a little bridge they were crossing, and seated himself firmly, leaving a place for her.

'But I want to get home-along,' dear Jim, she coaxed.

'Fidgets. Sit down, there' s a dear. I want a straightforward answer, if you please. In what month, and on what day of the month, will you marry me?'

'O, Jim,' she said, sitting gingerly on the edge, 'that' s too plain-spoken for you yet. Before I look at it in that business light I should have to—to—'

'But your father has settled it long ago, and you said it should be as soon as I became a partner. So, dear, you must not mind a plain man wanting a plain answer. Come, name your time.'
She did not reply at once. What thoughts were passing through her brain during the interval? Not images raised by his words, but whirling figures of men and women in red and white and blue, reflected from a glassy floor, in movements timed by the thrilling beats of the Drum Polka. At last she said slowly, 'Jim, you don' t know the world, and what a woman' s wants can be.'

'But I can make you comfortable. I am in lodgings as yet, but I can have a house for the asking; and as to furniture, you shall choose of the best for yourself—the very best.'

'The best! Far are you from knowing what that is!' said the little woman. 'There be ornaments such as you never dream of; work-tables that would set you in amaze; silver candlesticks, tea and coffee pots that would dazzle your eyes; tea-cups, and saucers, gilded all over with guinea-gold; heavy velvet curtains, gold clocks, pictures, and looking-glasses beyond your very dreams. So don't say I shall have the best.'

'H'm!' said Jim gloomily; and fell into reflection. 'Where did you get those high notions from, Margery?' he presently inquired.

'I'll swear you hadn't got 'em a week ago.' She did not answer, and he added, '*Yew* don't expect to have such things, I hope; deserve them as you may?'

'I was not exactly speaking of what I wanted,' she said severely. 'I said, things a woman *could* want. And since you wish to know what I *can* want to quite satisfy me, I assure you I can want those!'

'You are a pink-and-white conundrum, Margery,' he said; 'and I give you up for to-night. Anybody would think the devil had showed you all the kingdoms of the world since I saw you last!'

She reddened. 'Perhaps he has!' she murmured; then arose, he following her; and they soon reached Margery's home, approaching it from the lower or meadow side—the opposite to that of the garden top, where she had met the Baron.

'You'll come in, won't you, Jim?' she said, with more ceremony than heartiness.

'No—I think not to-night,' he answered. 'I'll consider what you've said.'

'You are very good, Jim,' she returned lightly. 'Good-bye.'

CHAPTER VII.

Jim thoughtfully retraced his steps. He was a village character, and he had a villager's simplicity: that is, the simplicity which comes from the lack of a complicated experience. But simple by nature he certainly was not. Among the rank and file of rustics he was quite a Talleyrand, or rather had been one, till he lost a good deal of his self-command by falling in love.

Now, however, that the charming object of his distraction was out of sight he could deliberate, and measure, and weigh things with some approach to keenness. The substance of his queries was, What change had come over Margery—whence these new notions?

Ponder as he would he could evolve no answer save one, which, eminently unsatisfactory as it was, he felt it would be unreasonable not to accept: that she was simply skittish and ambitious by nature, and would not be hunted into matrimony till he had provided a well-adorned home.

Jim retrod the miles to the kiln, and looked to the fires. The kiln stood in a peculiar, interesting, even impressive spot. It was at the end of a short ravine in a limestone formation, and all around was an open hilly down. The nearest house was that of Jim's cousin and partner, which stood on the outskirts of the down beside the turnpike-road. From this house a little lane wound between the steep escarpments of the ravine till it reached the kiln, which faced down the miniature valley, commanding it as a fort might command a defile.

The idea of a fort in this association owed little to imagination. For on the nibbled green steep above the kiln stood a bye-gone, worn-out specimen of such an erection, huge, impressive, and difficult to scale even now in its decay. It was a British castle or entrenchment, with triple rings of defence, rising roll behind roll, their outlines cutting sharply against the sky, and Jim's kiln nearly undermining their base. When the lime-kiln flared up in the night, which it often did, its fires lit up the front of these ramparts to a great majesty. They were old friends of his, and while keeping up the heat through the long darkness, as it was sometimes his duty to do, he would imagine the dancing lights and shades about the stupendous earthwork to be the forms of those giants who (he supposed) had heaped it up. Often he clambered upon it, and walked about the summit, thinking out the problems connected with his business, his partner, his future, his Margery.

It was what he did this evening, continuing the meditation on the young girl's manner that he had begun upon the road, and still, as then, finding no clue to the change.

While thus engaged he observed a man coming up the ravine to the kiln. Business messages were almost invariably left at the house below, and Jim watched the man with the interest excited by a belief that he had come on a personal matter. On nearer approach Jim recognized him as the gardener at Mount Lodge some miles away. If this meant business, the Baron (of whose arrival Jim had vaguely heard) was a new and unexpected customer.

It meant nothing else, apparently. The man's errand was simply to inform Jim that the Baron required a load of lime for the garden.

'You might have saved yourself trouble by leaving word at Mr. Vine's,' said Jim.

'I was to see you personally,' said the gardener, 'and to say that the Baron would like to inquire of you about the different qualities of lime proper for such purposes.'

'Couldn't you tell him yourself?' said Jim.

'He said I was to tell you that,' replied the gardener; 'and it wasn't for me to interfere.'

No motive other than the ostensible one could possibly be conjectured by Jim Hayward at this time; and the next morning he started with great pleasure, in his best business suit of clothes. By eleven o' clock he and his horse and cart had arrived on the Baron' s premises, and the lime was deposited where directed; an exceptional spot, just within view of the windows of the south front.

Baron von Xanten, pale and melancholy, was sauntering in the sun on the slope between the house and the all-the-year-round. He looked across to where Jim and the gardener were standing, and the identity of Hayward being established by what he brought, the Baron came down, and the gardener withdrew.

The Baron' s first inquiries were, as Jim had been led to suppose they would be, on the exterminating effects of lime upon slugs and snails in its different conditions of slaked and unslaked, ground and in the lump. He appeared to be much interested by Jim' s explanations, and eyed the young man closely whenever he had an opportunity.

'And I hope trade is prosperous with you this year,' said the Baron.

'Very, my noble lord,' replied Jim, who, in his uncertainty on the proper method of address, wisely concluded that it was better to err by giving too much honour than by giving too little. 'In short, trade is looking so well that I' ve become a partner in the firm.'

'Indeed; I am glad to hear it. So now you are settled in life.'

'Well, my lord; I am hardly settled, even now. For I' ve got to finish it—I mean, to get married.'

'That' s an easy matter, compared with the partnership.'

'Now a man might think so, my baron,' said Jim, getting more confidential. 'But the real truth is, ' tis the hardest part of all for me.'

'Your suit prospers, I hope?'

'It don' t,' said Jim. 'It don' t at all just at present. In short, I can' t for the life o' me think what' s come over the young woman lately.' And he fell into deep reflection.

Though Jim did not observe it, the Baron' s brow became shadowed with self-reproach as he heard those simple words, and his eyes had a look of pity. 'Indeed—since when?' he asked.

'Since yesterday, my noble lord.' Jim spoke meditatively. He was resolving upon a bold stroke. Why not make a confidant of this kind gentleman, instead of the parson, as he had intended? The thought was no sooner conceived than acted on. 'My lord,' he resumed, 'I have heard that you are a nobleman of great scope and talent, who has seen more strange countries and characters than I have ever heard of, and know the insides of men well. Therefore I would fain put a question to your noble lordship, if I may so trouble you, and having nobody else in the world who could inform me so trewly.'

'Any advice I can give is at your service, Hayward. What do you wish to know?'

'It is this, my baron. What can I do to bring down a young woman's ambition that's got to such a towering height there's no reaching it or compassing it: how get her to be pleased with me and my station as she used to be when I first knew her?'

'Truly, that's a hard question, my man. What does she aspire to?'

'She's got a craze for fine furniture.'

'How long has she had it?'

'Only just now.'

The Baron seemed still more to experience regret.

'What furniture does she specially covet?' he asked.

'Silver candlesticks, work-tables, looking-glasses, gold tea-things, silver tea-pots, gold clocks, curtains, pictures, and I don't know what all—things I shall never get if I live to be a hundred—not so much that I couldn't raise the money to buy 'em, as that to put it to other uses, or save it for a rainy day.'

'You think the possession of those articles would make her happy?'

'I really think they might, my lord.'

'Good. Open your pocket-book and write as I tell you.'

Jim in some astonishment did as commanded, and elevating his pocket-book against the garden-wall, thoroughly moistened his pencil, and wrote at the Baron's dictation:

'Pair of silver candlesticks: inlaid work-table and work-box: one large mirror: two small ditto: one gilt china tea and coffee service: one silver tea-pot, coffee-pot, sugar-basin, jug, and dozen spoons: French clock: pair of curtains: six large pictures.'

'Now,' said the Baron, 'tear out that leaf and give it to me. Keep a close tongue about this; go home, and don't be surprised at anything that may come to your door.'

'But, my noble lord, you don't mean that your lordship is going to give—'

'Never mind what I am going to do. Only keep your own counsel. I perceive that, though a plain countryman, you are by no means deficient in tact and understanding. If sending these things to you gives me pleasure, why should you object? The fact is, Hayward, I occasionally take an interest in people, and like to do a little for them. I take an interest in you. Now go home, and a week hence invite Marg—the young woman and her father, to tea with you. The rest is in your own hands.'

A question often put to Jim in after times was why it had not occurred to him at once that the Baron's liberal conduct must have been dictated by something more personal than sudden spontaneous generosity to him, a stranger. To which Jim always answered that, admitting the existence of such generosity, there had appeared nothing remarkable in the Baron selecting himself as its object. The Baron had told him that he took an interest in him; and self-esteem, even with the most modest, is usually sufficient to over-ride any little difficulty that might occur to an outsider in accounting for a preference. He moreover considered that foreign noblemen, rich and eccentric, might have habits of acting which were quite at variance with those of their English compeers.

So he drove off homeward with a lighter heart than he had known for several days. To have a foreign gentleman take a fancy to him—what a triumph to a plain sort of fellow, who had scarcely expected the Baron to look in his face. It would be a fine story to tell Margery when the Baron gave him liberty to speak out.

Jim lodged at the house of his cousin and partner, Richard Vine, a widower of fifty odd years. Having failed in the development of a household of direct descendants this tradesman had been glad to let his chambers to his much younger relative, when the latter entered on the business of lime manufacture; and their intimacy had led to a partnership. Jim lived upstairs; his partner lived down, and the furniture of all the rooms was so plain and old fashioned as to excite the special dislike of Miss Margery Tucker, and even to prejudice her against Jim for tolerating it. Not only were the chairs and tables queer, but, with due regard to the principle that a man's surroundings should bear the impress of that man's life and occupation, the chief ornaments of the dwelling were a curious collection of calcinations, that had been discovered from time to time in the lime-kiln—misshapen ingots of strange substance, some of them like Pompeian remains.

The head of the firm was a quiet-living, narrow-minded, though friendly, man of fifty; and he took a serious interest in Jim's love-suit, frequently inquiring how it progressed, and assuring Jim that if he chose to marry he might have all the upper floor at a low rent, he, Mr. Vine, contenting himself entirely with the ground level. It had been so convenient for discussing business matters to have Jim in the same house, that he did not wish any change to be made in consequence of a change in Jim's domestic estate. Margery knew of this wish, and of Jim's concurrent feeling; and did not like the idea at all.

About four days after the young man's interview with the Baron, there drew up in front of Jim's house at noon a waggon laden with cases and packages, large and small. They were all addressed to 'Mr. Hayward,' and they had come from the largest furnishing ware-houses in that part of England.

Three-quarters of an hour were occupied in getting the cases to Jim's rooms. The wary Jim did not show the amazement he felt at his patron's munificence; and presently the senior partner came into the passage, and wondered what was lumbering upstairs.

'Oh—it's only some things of mine,' said Jim coolly.

'Bearing upon the coming event—eh?' said his partner.

'Exactly,' replied Jim.

Mr. Vine, with some astonishment at the number of cases, shortly after went away to the kiln; whereupon Jim shut himself into his rooms, and there he might have been heard ripping up and opening boxes with a cautious hand, afterwards appearing outside the door with them empty, and carrying them off to the outhouse.

A triumphant look lit up his face when, a little later in the afternoon, he sent into the vale to the dairy, and invited Margery and her father to his house to supper.

She was not unsociable that day, and, her father expressing a hard and fast acceptance of the invitation, she perforce agreed to go with him. Meanwhile at home, Jim made himself as mysteriously busy as before in those rooms of his, and when his partner returned he too was asked to join in the supper.

At dusk Hayward went to the door, where he stood till he heard the voices of his guests from the direction of the low grounds, now covered with their frequent fleece of fog. The voices grew more distinct, and then on the white surface of the fog there appeared two trunkless heads, from which bodies and a horse and cart gradually extended as the approaching pair rose towards the house.

When they had entered Jim pressed Margery's hand and conducted her up to his rooms, her father waiting below to say a few words to the senior lime-burner.

'Bless me,' said Jim to her, on entering the sitting-room; 'I quite forgot to get a light beforehand; but I'll have one in a jiffy.'

33

Margery stood in the middle of the dark room, while Jim struck a match; and then the young girl's eyes were conscious of a burst of light, and the rise into being of a pair of handsome silver candlesticks containing two candles that Jim was in the act of lighting.

'Why—where—you have candlesticks like that?' said Margery. Her eyes flew round the room as the growing candle-flames showed other articles. 'Pictures too—and lovely china—why I knew nothing of this, I declare.'

'Yes—a few things that came to me by accident,' said Jim in quiet tones.

'And a great gold clock under a glass, and a cupid swinging for a pendulum; and O what a lovely work-table—woods of every colour—and a work-box to match. May I look inside that work-box, Jim?—whose is it?'

'O yes; look at it, of course. It is a poor enough thing, but ' tis mine; and it will belong to the woman I marry, whoever she may be, as well as all the other things here.'

'And the curtains and the looking-glasses: why I declare I can see myself in a hundred places.'

'That tea-set,' said Jim, placidly pointing to a gorgeous china service and a large silver tea-pot on the side table, 'I don't use at present, being a bachelor-man; but, says I to myself, "whoever I marry will want some such things for giving her parties; or I can sell em" —but I haven't took steps for't yet—'

'Sell ' em—no, I should think not,' said Margery with earnest reproach. 'Why, I hope you wouldn't be so foolish! Why, this is exactly the kind of thing I was thinking of when I told you of the things women could want—of course not meaning myself particularly. I had no idea that you had such valuable—'

Margery was unable to speak coherently, so much was she amazed at the wealth of Jim's possessions.

At this moment her father and the lime-burner came upstairs; and to appear womanly and proper to Mr. Vine, Margery repressed the remainder of her surprise.

As for the two elderly worthies, it was not till they entered the room and sat down that their slower eyes discerned anything brilliant in the appointments. Then one of them stole a glance at some article, and the other at another; but each being unwilling to express his wonder in the presence of his neighbours, they received the objects before them with quite an accustomed air; the lime-burner inwardly trying to conjecture what all this meant, and the dairyman musing that if Jim's business allowed him to accumulate at this rate, the sooner Margery became his wife the better. Margery retreated to the work-table, work-box, and tea-service, which she examined with hushed exclamations.

An entertainment thus surprisingly begun could not fail to progress well. Whenever Margery's crusty old father felt the need of a civil sentence, the flash of Jim's fancy articles inspired him to one; while the lime-burner, having reasoned away his first ominous thought that all this had come out of the firm, also felt proud and blithe.

Jim accompanied his dairy friends part of the way home before they mounted. Her father, finding that Jim wanted to speak to her privately, and that she exhibited some elusiveness, turned to Margery and said;

'Come, come, my lady; no more of this nonsense. You just step behind with that young man, and I and the cart will wait for you.'

Margery, a little scared at her father's peremptoriness, obeyed. It was plain that Jim had won the old man by that night's stroke, if he had not won her.

'I know what you are going to say, Jim,' she began, less ardently now, for she was no longer under the novel influence of the shining silver and glass. 'Well, as you desire it, and as my father desires it, and as I suppose it will be the best course for me, I will fix the day—not this evening, but as soon as I can think it over.'

CHAPTER VIII.

Notwithstanding a press of business, Jim went and did his duty in thanking the Baron. The latter saw him in his fishing-tackle room, an apartment littered with every appliance that a votary of the rod could require.

'And when is the wedding-day to be, Hayward?' the Baron asked, after Jim had told him that matters were settled.

'It is not quite certain yet, my noble lord,' said Jim cheerfully. 'But I hope 'twill not be long after the time when God A' mighty christens the little apples.'

'And when is that?'

'St. Swithin's—the middle of July. 'Tis to be some time in that month, she tells me.'

When Jim was gone the Baron seemed meditative. He went out, ascended the mount, and entered the weather-screen, where he looked at the seats, as though re-enacting in his fancy the scene of that memorable morning of fog. He turned his eyes to the angle of the shelter, round which Margery had suddenly appeared like a vision, and it was plain that he would not have minded her appearing there then. The juncture had indeed been such an impressive and critical one that she must have seemed rather a heavenly messenger than a passing milkmaid, more especially to a man like the Baron, who, despite the mystery of his origin and life, revealed himself to be a melancholy, emotional character—the Jacques of this forest and stream.

Behind the mount the ground rose yet higher, ascending to a plantation which sheltered the house. The Baron strolled up here, and bent his gaze over the distance. The valley of the Exe lay before him, with its shining river, the brooks that fed it, and the trickling springs that fed the brooks. The situation of Margery's house was visible, though not the house itself; and the Baron gazed that way for an infinitely long time, till, remembering himself, he moved on.

Instead of returning to the house he went along the ridge till he arrived at the verge of Chillington Wood, and in the same desultory manner roamed under the trees, not pausing till he had come to Three-Walks-End, and the hollow elm hard by. He peeped in at the rift. In the soft dry layer of touch-wood that floored the hollow Margery's tracks were still visible, as she had made them there when dressing for the ball.

'Little Margery!' murmured the Baron.

In a moment he thought better of this mood, and turned to go home. But behold, a form stood behind him—that of the girl whose name had been on his lips.

She was in utter confusion. 'I—I—did not know you were here, sir!' she began. 'I was out for a little walk.' She could get no further; her eyes filled with tears. That spice of wilfulness, even hardness, which characterized her in Jim's company, magically disappeared in the presence of the Baron.

'Never mind, never mind,' said he, masking under a severe manner whatever he felt. 'The meeting is awkward, and ought not to have occurred, especially if as I suppose, you are shortly to be married to James Hayward. But it cannot be helped now. You had no idea I was here, of course. Neither had I of seeing you. Remember you cannot be too careful,' continued the Baron, in the same grave tone; 'and I strongly request you as a friend to do your utmost to avoid meetings like this. When you saw me before I turned, why did you not go away?'

'I did not see you, sir. I did not think of seeing you. I was walking this way, and I only looked in to see the tree.'

'That shows you have been thinking of things you should not think of,' returned the Baron. 'Good morning.'

Margery could answer nothing. A browbeaten glance, almost of misery, was all she gave him. He took a slow step away from her; then turned suddenly back and, stooping, impulsively kissed her cheek, taking her as much by surprise as ever a woman was taken in her life.

Immediately after he went off with a flushed face and rapid strides, which he did not check till he was within his own boundaries.

The haymaking season now set in vigorously, and the weir-hatches were all drawn in the meads to drain off the water. The streams ran themselves dry, and there was no longer any difficulty in walking about among them. The Baron could very well witness from the elevations about his house the activity which followed these preliminaries. The white shirt-sleeves of the mowers glistened in the sun, the scythes flashed, voices echoed, snatches of song floated about, and there were glimpses of red waggon-wheels, purple gowns, and many-coloured handkerchiefs.

The Baron had been told that the haymaking was to be followed by the wedding, and had he gone down the vale to the dairy he would have had evidence to that effect. Dairyman Tucker's house was in a whirlpool of bustle, and among other difficulties was that of turning the cheese-room into a genteel apartment for the time being, and hiding the awkwardness of having to pass through the milk-house to get to the parlour door. These household contrivances appeared to interest Margery much more than the great question of dressing for the ceremony and the ceremony itself. In all relating to that she showed an indescribable backwardness, which later on was well remembered.

'If it were only somebody else, and I was one of the bridesmaids, I really think I should like it better!' she murmured one afternoon.

'Away with thee—that's only your shyness!' said one of the milkmaids.

It is said that about this time the Baron seemed to feel the effects of solitude strongly. Solitude revives the simple instincts of primitive man, and lonely country nooks afford rich soil for wayward emotions. Moreover, idleness waters those unconsidered impulses which a short season of turmoil would stamp out. It is difficult to speak with any exactness of the bearing of such conditions on the mind of the Baron—a man of whom so little was ever truly known—but there is no doubt that his mind ran much on Margery as an individual, without reference to her rank or quality, or to the question whether she would marry Jim Hayward that summer. She was the single lovely human thing within his present horizon, for he lived in absolute seclusion; and her image unduly affected him.

But, leaving conjecture, let me state what happened.

One Saturday evening, two or three weeks after his accidental meeting with her in the wood, he wrote the note following:—

DEAR MARGERY,—

You must not suppose that, because I spoke somewhat severely to you at our chance encounter by the hollow tree, I have any feeling against you. Far from it. Now, as ever, I have the most grateful sense of your considerate kindness to me on a momentous occasion which shall be nameless.

You solemnly promised to come and see me whenever I should send for you. Can you call for five minutes as soon as possible, and disperse those plaguy glooms from which I am so unfortunate as to suffer? If you refuse I will not answer for the consequences.

I shall be in the summer shelter of the mount to-morrow morning at half-past ten. If you come I shall be grateful. I have also something for you.

Yours,
X.

In keeping with the tenor of this epistle the desponding, self-oppressed Baron ascended the mount on Sunday morning and sat down. There was nothing here to signify exactly the hour, but before the church bells had begun he heard somebody approaching at the back. The light footstep moved timidly, first to one recess, and then to another; then to the third, where he sat in the shade. Poor Margery stood before him.

She looked worn and weary, and her little shoes and the skirts of her dress were covered with dust. The weather was sultry, the sun being already high and powerful, and rain had not fallen for weeks. The Baron, who walked little, had thought nothing of the effects of this heat and drought in inducing fatigue. A distance which had been but a reasonable exercise on a foggy morning was a drag for Margery now. She was out of breath; and anxiety, even unhappiness was written on her everywhere. He rose to his feet, and took her hand. He was vexed with himself at sight of her. 'My dear little girl!' he said. 'You are tired—you should not have come.'

'You sent for me, sir; and I was afraid you were ill; and my promise to you was sacred.'

He bent over her, looking upon her downcast face, and still holding her hand; then he dropped it, and took a pace or two backwards.

'It was a whim, nothing more,' he said, sadly. 'I wanted to see my little friend, to express good wishes—and to present her with this.' He held forward a small morocco case, and showed her how to open it, disclosing a pretty locket, set with pearls. 'It is intended as a wedding present,' he continued. 'To be returned to me again if you do not marry Jim this summer—it is to be this summer, I think?'

'It was, sir,' she said with agitation. 'But it is so no longer. And, therefore, I cannot take this.'

'What do you say?'

'It was to have been to-day; but now it cannot be.'

'The wedding to-day—Sunday?' he cried.

'We fixed Sunday not to hinder much time at this busy season of the year,' replied she.

'And have you, then, put it off—surely not?'

'You sent for me, and I have come,' she answered humbly, like an obedient familiar in the employ of some great enchanter. Indeed, the Baron's power over this innocent girl was curiously like enchantment, or mesmeric influence. It was so masterful that the sexual element was almost eliminated. It was that of Prospero over the gentle Ariel. And yet it was probably only that of the cosmopolite over the recluse, of the experienced man over the simple maid.

'You have come—on your wedding-day!—O Margery, this is a mistake. Of course, you should not have obeyed me, since, though I thought your wedding would be soon, I did not know it was to-day.'

'I promised you, sir; and I would rather keep my promise to you than be married to Jim.'

'That must not be—the feeling is wrong!' he murmured, looking at the distant hills. 'There seems to be a fate in all this; I get out of the frying-pan into the fire. What a recompense to you for your goodness! The fact is, I was out of health and out of spirits, so I—but no more of that. Now instantly to repair this tremendous blunder that we have made—that's the question.'

After a pause, he went on hurriedly, 'Walk down the hill; get into the road. By that time I shall be there with a phaeton. We may get back in time. What time is it now? If not, no doubt the wedding can be to-morrow; so all will come right again. Don't cry, my dear girl. Keep the locket, of course—you'll marry Jim.'

CHAPTER IX.

He hastened down towards the stables, and she went on as directed. It seemed as if he must have put in the horse himself, so quickly did he reappear with the phaeton on the open road. Margery silently took her seat, and the Baron seemed cut to the quick with self-reproach as he noticed the listless indifference with which she acted. There was no doubt that in her heart she had preferred obeying the apparently important mandate that morning to becoming Jim's wife; but there was no less doubt that had the Baron left her alone she would quietly have gone to the altar.

He drove along furiously, in a cloud of dust. There was much to contemplate in that peaceful Sunday morning—the windless trees and fields, the shaking sunlight, the pause in human stir. Yet neither of them heeded, and thus they drew near to the dairy. His first expressed intention had been to go indoors with her, but this he abandoned as impolitic in the highest degree.

'You may be soon enough,' he said, springing down, and helping her to follow. 'Tell the truth: say you were sent for to receive a wedding present—that it was a mistake on my part—a mistake on yours; and I think they'll forgive . . . And, Margery, my last request to you is this: that if I send for you again, you do not come. Promise solemnly, my dear girl, that any such request shall be unheeded.'

Her lips moved, but the promise was not articulated. 'O, sir, I cannot promise it!' she said at last.

'But you must; your salvation may depend on it!' he insisted almost sternly. 'You don't know what I am.'

'Then, sir, I promise,' she replied. 'Now leave me to myself, please, and I'll go indoors and manage matters.'

He turned the horse and drove away, but only for a little distance. Out of sight he pulled rein suddenly. 'Only to go back and propose it to her, and she'd come!' he murmured.

He stood up in the phaeton, and by this means he could see over the hedge. Margery still sat listlessly in the same place; there was not a lovelier flower in the field. 'No,' he said; 'no, no—never!' He reseated himself, and the wheels sped lightly back over the soft dust to Mount Lodge.

Meanwhile Margery had not moved. If the Baron could dissimulate on the side of severity she could dissimulate on the side of calm. He did not know what had been veiled by the quiet promise to manage matters indoors. Rising at length she first turned away from the house; and, by-and-by, having apparently forgotten till then that she carried it in her hand, she opened the case, and looked at the locket. This seemed to give her courage. She turned, set her face towards the dairy in good earnest, and though her heart faltered when the gates came in sight, she kept on and drew near the door.

On the threshold she stood listening. The house was silent. Decorations were visible in the passage, and also the carefully swept and sanded path to the gate, which she was to have trodden as a bride; but the sparrows hopped over it as if it were abandoned; and all appeared to have been checked at its climacteric, like a clock stopped on the strike. Till this moment of confronting the suspended animation of the scene she had not realized the full shock of the convulsion which her disappearance must have caused. It is quite certain—apart from her own repeated assurances to that effect in later years—that in hastening off that morning to her sudden engagement, Margery had not counted the cost of such an enterprise; while a dim notion that she might get back again in time for the ceremony, if the message meant nothing serious, should also be mentioned in her favour. But, upon the whole, she had obeyed the call with an unreasoning obedience worthy of a disciple in primitive times. A conviction that the Baron's life might depend upon her presence—for she had by this time divined the tragical event she had interrupted on the foggy morning—took from her all will to judge and consider calmly. The simple affairs of her and hers seemed nothing beside the possibility of harm to him.

A well-known step moved on the sanded floor within, and she went forward. That she saw her father's face before her, just within the door, can hardly be said: it was rather Reproach and Rage in a human mask.

'What! ye have dared to come back alive, hussy, to look upon the dupery you have practised on honest people! You've mortified us all; I don't want to see 'ee; I don't want to hear 'ee; I don't want to know anything!' He walked up and down the room, unable to command himself. 'Nothing but being dead could have excused 'ee for not meeting and marrying that man this morning; and yet you have the brazen impudence to stand there as well as ever! What be you here for?'

'I've come back to marry Jim, if he wants me to,' she said faintly.

'And if not—perhaps so much the better. I was sent for this morning early. I thought—.' She halted. To say that she had thought a man's death might happen by his own hand if she did not go to him, would never do. 'I was obliged to go,' she said. 'I had given my word.'

'Why didn't you tell us then, so that the wedding could be put off, without making fools o' us?'

'Because I was afraid you wouldn't let me go, and I had made up my mind to go.'

'To go where?'

She was silent; till she said, 'I will tell Jim all, and why it was; and if he's any friend of mine he'll excuse me.'

'Not Jim—he's no such fool. Jim had put all ready for you, Jim had called at your house, a-dressed up in his new wedding clothes, and a-smiling like the sun; Jim had told the parson, had got the ringers in tow, and the clerk awaiting; and then—you was *gone*! Then Jim turned as pale as rendlewood, and busted out, "If she don't marry me to-day," 'a said, "she don't marry me at all! No; let her look elsewhere for a husband. For tew years I've put up with her haughty tricks and her takings," 'a said. "I've droudged and I've traipsed, I've bought and I've sold, all wi' an eye to her; I've suffered horseflesh," he says—yes, them was his noble words— "but I'll suffer it no longer. She shall go!" "Jim," says I, "you be a man. If she's alive, I commend 'ee; if she's dead, pity my old age." "She isn't dead," says he; "for I've just heard she was seen walking off across the fields this morning, looking all of a scornful triumph." He turned round and went, and the rest o' the neighbours went; and here be I left to the reproach o' t.'

'He was too hasty,' murmured Margery. 'For now he's said this I can't marry him to-morrow, as I might ha' done; and perhaps so much the better.'

'You can be so calm about it, can ye? Be my arrangements nothing, then, that you should break 'em up, and say off hand what wasn't done to-day might ha' been done to-morrow, and such flick-flack? Out o' my sight! I won't hear any more. I won't speak to 'ee any more.'

'I'll go away, and then you'll be sorry!'

'Very well, go. Sorry—not I.'

He turned and stamped his way into the cheese-room. Margery went upstairs. She too was excited now, and instead of fortifying herself in her bedroom till her father's rage had blown over, as she had often done on lesser occasions, she packed up a bundle of articles, crept down again, and went out of the house. She had a place of refuge in these cases of necessity, and her father knew it, and was less alarmed at seeing her depart than he might otherwise have been. This place was Rook's Gate, the house of her grandmother, who always took Margery's part when that young woman was particularly in the wrong.

The devious way she pursued, to avoid the vicinity of Mount Lodge, was tedious, and she was already weary. But the cottage was a restful place to arrive at, for she was her own mistress there—her grandmother never coming down stairs—and Edy, the woman who lived with and attended her, being a cipher except in muscle and voice. The approach was by a straight open road, bordered by thin lank trees, all sloping away from the south-west wind-quarter, and the scene bore a strange resemblance to certain bits of Dutch landscape which have been imprinted on the world's eye by Hobbema and his school.

Having explained to her granny that the wedding was put off; and that she had come to stay, one of Margery's first acts was carefully to pack up the locket and case, her wedding present from the Baron. The conditions of the gift were unfulfilled, and she wished it to go back instantly. Perhaps, in the intricacies of her bosom, there lurked a greater satisfaction with the reason for returning the present than she would have felt just then with a reason for keeping it.

To send the article was difficult. In the evening she wrapped herself up, searched and found a gauze veil that had been used by her grandmother in past years for hiving swarms of bees, buried her face in it, and sallied forth with a palpitating heart till she drew near the tabernacle of her demi-god the Baron. She ventured only to the back-door, where she handed in the parcel addressed to him, and quickly came away.

Now it seems that during the day the Baron had been unable to learn the result of his attempt to return Margery in time for the event he had interrupted. Wishing, for obvious reasons, to avoid direct inquiry by messenger, and being too unwell to go far himself, he could learn no particulars. He was sitting in thought after a lonely dinner when the parcel intimating failure as brought in. The footman, whose curiosity had been excited by the mode of its arrival, peeped through the keyhole after closing the door, to learn what the packet meant. Directly the Baron had opened it he thrust out his feet vehemently from his chair, and began cursing his ruinous conduct in bringing about such a disaster, for the return of the locket denoted not only no wedding that day, but none to-morrow, or at any time.

'I have done that innocent woman a great wrong!' he murmured.

'Deprived her of, perhaps, her only opportunity of becoming mistress of a happy home!'

CHAPTER X.

A considerable period of inaction followed among all concerned. Nothing tended to dissipate the obscurity which veiled the life of the

Baron. The position he occupied in the minds of the country-folk around was one which combined the mysteriousness of a legendary character with the unobtrusive deeds of a modern gentleman. To this day whoever takes the trouble to go down to Silverthorn in Lower Wessex and make inquiries will find existing there almost a superstitious feeling for the moody melancholy stranger who resided in the Lodge some forty years ago.

Whence he came, whither he was going, were alike unknown. It was said that his mother had been an English lady of noble family who had married a foreigner not unheard of in circles where men pile up 'the cankered heaps of strange-achieved gold' —that he had been born and educated in England, taken abroad, and so on. But the facts of a life in such cases are of little account beside the aspect of a life; and hence, though doubtless the years of his existence contained their share of trite and homely circumstance, the curtain which masked all this was never lifted to gratify such a theatre of spectators as those at Silverthorn. Therein lay his charm. His life was a vignette, of which the central strokes only were drawn with any distinctness, the environment shading away to a blank.

He might have been said to resemble that solitary bird the heron. The still, lonely stream was his frequent haunt: on its banks he would stand for hours with his rod, looking into the water, beholding the tawny inhabitants with the eye of a philosopher, and seeming to say, 'Bite or don' t bite—it' s all the same to me.' He was often mistaken for a ghost by children; and for a pollard willow by men, when, on their way home in the dusk, they saw him motionless by some rushy bank, unobservant of the decline of day.

Why did he come to fish near Silverthorn? That was never explained. As far as was known he had no relatives near; the fishing there was not exceptionally good; the society thereabout was decidedly meagre. That he had committed some folly or hasty act, that he had been wrongfully accused of some crime, thus rendering his seclusion from the world desirable for a while, squared very well with his frequent melancholy. But such as he was there he lived, well supplied with fishing-tackle, and tenant of a furnished house, just suited to the requirements of such an eccentric being as he.

Margery' s father, having privately ascertained that she was living with her grandmother, and getting into no harm, refrained from communicating with her, in the hope of seeing her contrite at his door. It had, of course, become known about Silverthorn that at the last moment Margery refused to wed Hayward, by absenting herself from the house.

Jim was pitied, yet not pitied much, for it was said that he ought not to have been so eager for a woman who had shown no anxiety for him. And where was Jim himself? It must not be supposed that that tactician had all this while withdrawn from mortal eye to tear his hair in silent indignation and despair. He had, in truth, merely retired up the lonesome defile between the downs to his smouldering kiln, and the ancient ramparts above it; and there, after his first hours of natural discomposure, he quietly waited for overtures from the possibly repentant Margery. But no overtures arrived, and then he meditated anew on the absorbing problem of her skittishness, and how to set about another campaign for her conquest, notwithstanding his late disastrous failure. Why had he failed? To what was her strange conduct owing? That was the thing which puzzled him.

He had made no advance in solving the riddle when, one morning, a stranger appeared on the down above him, looking as if he had lost his way. The man had a good deal of black hair below his felt hat, and carried under his arm a case containing a musical instrument. Descending to where Jim stood, he asked if there were not a short cut across that way to Tivworthy, where a fête was to be held.

'Well, yes, there is,' said Jim. 'But ' tis an enormous distance for ' ee.'

'Oh, yes,' replied the musician. 'I wish to intercept the carrier on the highway.'

The nearest way was precisely in the direction of Rook' s Gate, where Margery, as Jim knew, was staying. Having some time to spare, Jim was strongly impelled to make a kind act to the lost musician a pretext for taking observations in that neighbourhood, and telling his acquaintance that he was going the same way, he started without further ado.

They skirted the long length of meads, and in due time arrived at the back of Rook' s Gate, where the path joined the high road. A hedge divided the public way from the cottage garden. Jim drew up at this point and said, 'Your road is straight on: I turn back here.'

But the musician was standing fixed, as if in great perplexity. Thrusting his hand into his forest of black hair, he murmured, 'Surely it is the same—surely!'

Jim, following the direction of his neighbour' s eyes, found them to be fixed on a figure till that moment hidden from himself—Margery Tucker—who was crossing the garden to an opposite gate with a little cheese in her arms, her head thrown back, and her face quite exposed.

'What of her?' said Jim.

'Two months ago I formed one of the band at the Yeomanry Ball given by Lord Toneborough in the next county. I saw that young lady dancing the polka there in robes of gauze and lace. Now I see her carry a cheese!'

'Never!' said Jim incredulously.

'But I do not mistake. I say it is so!'

Jim ridiculed the idea; the bandsman protested, and was about to lose his temper, when Jim gave in with the good-nature of a person who can afford to despise opinions; and the musician went his way.

As he dwindled out of sight Jim began to think more carefully over what he had said. The young man's thoughts grew quite to an excitement, for there came into his mind the Baron's extraordinary kindness in regard to furniture, hitherto accounted for by the assumption that the nobleman had taken a fancy to him. Could it be, among all the amazing things of life, that the Baron was at the bottom of this mischief; and that he had amused himself by taking Margery to a ball?

Doubts and suspicions which distract some lovers to imbecility only served to bring out Jim's great qualities. Where he trusted he was the most trusting fellow in the world; where he doubted he could be guilty of the slyest strategy. Once suspicious, he became one of those subtle, watchful characters who, without integrity, make good thieves; with a little, good jobbers; with a little more, good diplomatists. Jim was honest, and he considered what to do.

Retracing his steps, he peeped again. She had gone in; but she would soon reappear, for it could be seen that she was carrying little new cheeses one by one to a spring-cart and horse tethered outside the gate— her grandmother, though not a regular dairywoman, still managing a few cows by means of a man and maid. With the lightness of a cat Jim crept round to the gate, took a piece of chalk from his pocket, and wrote upon the boarding 'The Baron.' Then he retreated to the other side of the garden where he had just watched Margery.

In due time she emerged with another little cheese, came on to the garden-door, and glanced upon the chalked words which confronted her. She started; the cheese rolled from her arms to the ground, and broke into pieces like a pudding.

She looked fearfully round, her face burning like sunset, and, seeing nobody, stooped to pick up the flaccid lumps. Jim, with a pale face, departed as invisibly as he had come. He had proved the bandsman's tale to be true. On his way back he formed a resolution. It was to beard the lion in his den—to call on the Baron.

Meanwhile Margery had recovered her equanimity, and gathered up the broken cheese. But she could by no means account for the handwriting. Jim was just the sort of fellow to play her such a trick at ordinary times, but she imagined him to be far too incensed against her to do it now; and she suddenly wondered if it were any sort of signal from the Baron himself.

Of him she had lately heard nothing. If ever monotony pervaded a life it pervaded hers at Rook's Gate; and she had begun to despair of any happy change. But it is precisely when the social atmosphere seems stagnant that great events are brewing. Margery's quiet was broken first, as we have seen, by a slight start, only sufficient to make her drop a cheese; and then by a more serious matter.

She was inside the same garden one day when she heard two watermen talking without. The conversation was to the effect that the strange gentleman who had taken Mount Lodge for the season was seriously ill.

'How ill?' cried Margery through the hedge, which screened her from recognition.

'Bad abed,' said one of the watermen.

'Inflammation of the lungs,' said the other.

'Got wet, fishing,' the first chimed in.

Margery could gather no more. An ideal admiration rather than any positive passion existed in her breast for the Baron: she had of late seen too little of him to allow any incipient views of him as a lover to grow to formidable dimensions. It was an extremely romantic feeling, delicate as an aroma, capable of quickening to an active principle, or dying to 'a painless sympathy,' as the case might be.

This news of his illness, coupled with the mysterious chalking on the gate, troubled her, and revived his image much. She took to walking up and down the garden-paths, looking into the hearts of flowers, and not thinking what they were. His last request had been that she was not to go to him if be should send for her; and now she asked herself, was the name on the gate a hint to enable her to go without infringing the letter of her promise? Thus unexpectedly had Jim's manœuvre operated.

Ten days passed. All she could hear of the Baron were the same words, 'Bad abed,' till one afternoon, after a gallop of the physician to the Lodge, the tidings spread like lightning that the Baron was dying. Margery distressed herself with the question whether she might be permitted to visit him and say her prayers at his bedside; but she feared to venture; and thus eight-and-forty hours slipped away, and the Baron still lived. Despite her shyness and awe of him she had almost made up her mind to call when, just at dusk on that October evening, somebody came to the door and asked for her.

47

She could see the messenger's head against the low new moon. He was a man-servant. He said he had been all the way to her father's, and had been sent thence to her here. He simply brought a note, and, delivering it into her hands, went away.

DEAR MARGERY TUCKER (ran the note)—They say I am not likely to live, so I want to see you. Be here at eight o'clock this evening. Come quite alone to the side-door, and tap four times softly. My trusty man will admit you. The occasion is an important one. Prepare yourself for a solemn ceremony, which I wish to have performed while it lies in my power.

VON XANTEN.

CHAPTER XI.

Margery's face flushed up, and her neck and arms glowed in sympathy. The quickness of youthful imagination, and the assumptiveness of woman's reason, sent her straight as an arrow this thought: 'He wants to marry me!'

She had heard of similar strange proceedings, in which the orange-flower and the sad cypress were intertwined. People sometimes wished on their death-beds, from motives of esteem, to form a legal tie which they had not cared to establish as a domestic one during their active life. For a few minutes Margery could hardly be called excited; she was excitement itself. Between surprise and modesty she blushed and trembled by turns. She became grave, sat down in the solitary room, and looked into the fire. At seven o'clock she rose resolved, and went quite tranquilly upstairs, where she speedily began to dress.

In making this hasty toilet nine-tenths of her care were given to her hands. The summer had left them slightly brown, and she held them up and looked at them with some misgiving, the fourth finger of her left hand more especially. Hot washings and cold washings, certain products from bee and flower known only to country girls, everything she could think of, were used upon those little sunburnt hands, till she persuaded herself that they were really as white as could be wished by a husband with a hundred titles. Her dressing completed, she left word with Edy that she was going for a long walk, and set out in the direction of Mount Lodge.

She no longer tripped like a girl, but walked like a woman. While crossing the park she murmured 'Baroness von Xanten' in a pronunciation of her own. The sound of that title caused her such agitation that she was obliged to pause, with her hand upon her heart. The house was so closely neighboured by shrubberies on three of its sides that it was not till she had gone nearly round it that she found the little door. The resolution she had been an hour in forming failed her when she stood at the portal. While pausing for courage to tap, a carriage drove up to the front entrance a little way off, and peeping round the corner she saw alight a clergyman, and a gentleman in whom Margery fancied that she recognized a well-known solicitor from the neighbouring town. She had no longer any doubt of the nature of the ceremony proposed.   'It is sudden but I must obey him!' she murmured: and tapped four times.

The door was opened so quickly that the servant must have been standing immediately inside. She thought him the man who had driven them to the ball—the silent man who could be trusted. Without a word he conducted her up the back staircase, and through a door at the top, into a wide corridor. She was asked to wait in a little dressing-room, where there was a fire, and an old metal-framed looking-glass over the mantel-piece, in which she caught sight of herself. A red spot burnt in each of her cheeks; the rest of her face was pale; and her eyes were like diamonds of the first water.

Before she had been seated many minutes the man came back noiselessly, and she followed him to a door covered by a red and black curtain, which he lifted, and ushered her into a large chamber. A screened light stood on a table before her, and on her left the hangings of a tall dark four-post bedstead obstructed her view of the centre of the room. Everything here seemed of such a magnificent type to her eyes that she felt confused, diminished to half her height, half her strength, half her prettiness. The man who had conducted her retired at once, and some one came softly round the angle of the bed-curtains. He held out his hand kindly—rather patronisingly: it was the solicitor whom she knew by sight. This gentleman led her forward, as if she had been a lamb rather than a woman, till the occupant of the bed was revealed.

The Baron's eyes were closed, and her entry had been so noiseless that he did not open them. The pallor of his face nearly matched the white bed-linen, and his dark hair and heavy black moustache were like dashes of ink on a clean page. Near him sat the parson and another gentleman, whom she afterwards learnt to be a London physician; and on the parson whispering a few words the Baron opened his eyes. As soon as he saw her he smiled faintly, and held out his hand.

Margery would have wept for him, if she had not been too overawed and palpitating to do anything. She quite forgot what she had come for, shook hands with him mechanically, and could hardly return an answer to his weak 'Dear Margery, you see how I am—how are you?'

In preparing for marriage she had not calculated on such a scene as this. Her affection for the Baron had too much of the vague in it to afford her trustfulness now. She wished she had not come. On a sign from the Baron the lawyer brought her a chair, and the oppressive silence was broken by the Baron's words.

'I am pulled down to death's door, Margery,' he said; 'and I suppose I soon shall pass through . . . My peace has been much disturbed in this illness, for just before it attacked me I received—that present you returned, from which, and in other ways, I learnt that you had lost your chance of marriage . . . Now it was I who did the harm, and you can imagine how the news has affected me. It has worried me all the illness through, and I cannot dismiss my error from my mind . . . I want to right the wrong I have done you before I die. Margery, you have always obeyed me, and, strange as the request may be, will you obey me now?'

She whispered 'Yes.'

'Well, then,' said the Baron, 'these three gentlemen are here for a special purpose: one helps the body—he's called a physician; another helps the soul—he's a parson; the other helps the understanding—he's a lawyer. They are here partly on my account, and partly on yours.'

The speaker then made a sign to the lawyer, who went out of the door. He came back almost instantly, but not alone. Behind him, dressed up in his best clothes, with a flower in his buttonhole and a bridegroom's air, walked—Jim.

CHAPTER XII.

Margery could hardly repress a scream. As for flushing and blushing, she had turned hot and turned pale so many times already during the evening, that there was really now nothing of that sort left for her to do; and she remained in complexion much as before. O, the mockery of it! That secret dream—that sweet word 'Baroness!'—which had sustained her all the way along. Instead of a Baron there stood Jim, white-waistcoated, demure, every hair in place, and, if she mistook not, even a deedy spark in his eye.

Jim's surprising presence on the scene may be briefly accounted for. His resolve to seek an explanation with the Baron at all risks had proved unexpectedly easy: the interview had at once been granted, and then, seeing the crisis at which matters stood, the Baron had generously revealed to Jim the whole of his indebtedness to and knowledge of Margery. The truth of the Baron's statement, the innocent nature as yet of the acquaintanceship, his sorrow for the rupture he had produced, was so evident that, far from having any further doubts of his patron, Jim frankly asked his advice on the next step to be pursued. At this stage the Baron fell ill, and, desiring much to see the two young people united before his death, he had sent anew Hayward, and proposed the plan which they were to now about to attempt—a marriage at the bedside of the sick man by special licence. The influence at Lambeth of some friends of the Baron's, and the charitable bequests of his late mother to several deserving Church funds, were generally supposed to be among the reasons why the application for the licence was not refused.

This, however, is of small consequence. The Baron probably knew, in proposing this method of celebrating the marriage, that his enormous power over her would outweigh any sentimental obstacles which she might set up—inward objections that, without his presence and firmness, might prove too much for her acquiescence. Doubtless he foresaw, too, the advantage of getting her into the house before making the individuality of her husband clear to her mind.

Now, the Baron's conjectures were right as to the event, but wrong as to the motives. Margery was a perfect little dissembler on some occasions, and one of them was when she wished to hide any sudden mortification that might bring her into ridicule. She had no sooner recovered from her first fit of discomfiture than pride bade her suffer anything rather than reveal her absurd disappointment. Hence the scene progressed as follows:

'Come here, Hayward,' said the invalid. Hayward came near. The Baron, holding her hand in one of his own, and her lover's in the other, continued, 'Will you, in spite of your recent vexation with her, marry her now if she does not refuse?'

'I will, sir,' said Jim promptly.

'And Margery, what do you say? It is merely a setting of things right. You have already promised this young man to be his wife, and should, of course, perform your promise. You don't dislike Jim?'

'O, no, sir,' she said, in a low, dry voice.

'I like him better than I can tell you,' said the Baron. 'He is an honourable man, and will make you a good husband. You must remember that marriage is a life contract, in which general compatibility of temper and worldly position is of more importance than fleeting passion, which never long survives. Now, will you, at my earnest request, and before I go to the South of Europe to die, agree to make this good man happy? I have expressed your views on the subject, haven't I, Hayward?'

'To a T, sir,' said Jim emphatically; with a motion of raising his hat to his influential ally, till he remembered he had no hat on. 'And, though I could hardly expect Margery to gie in for my asking, I feels she ought to gie in for yours.'

'And you accept him, my little friend?'

'Yes, sir,' she murmured, 'if he'll agree to a thing or two.'

'Doubtless he will—what are they?'

'That I shall not be made to live with him till I am in the mind for it; and that my having him shall be kept unknown for the present.'

'Well, what do you think of it, Hayward?'

'Anything that you or she may wish I'll do, my noble lord,' said Jim.

'Well, her request is not unreasonable, seeing that the proceedings are, on my account, a little hurried. So we'll proceed. You rather expected this, from my allusion to a ceremony in my note, did you not, Margery?'

'Yes, sir,' said she, with an effort.

'Good; I thought so; you looked so little surprised.'

We now leave the scene in the bedroom for a spot not many yards off. When the carriage seen by Margery at the door was driving up to Mount Lodge it arrested the attention, not only of the young girl, but of a man who had for some time been moving slowly about the opposite lawn, engaged in some operation while he smoked a short pipe. A short observation of his doings would have shown that he was sheltering some delicate plants from an expected frost, and that he was the gardener. When the light at the door fell upon the entering forms of parson and lawyer—the former a stranger, the latter known to him—the gardener walked thoughtfully round the house. Reaching the small side-entrance he was further surprised to see it noiselessly open to a young woman, in whose momentarily illumined features he discerned those of Margery Tucker.

Altogether there was something curious in this. The man returned to the lawn front, and perfunctorily went on putting shelters over certain plants, though his thoughts were plainly otherwise engaged. On the grass his footsteps were noiseless, and the night moreover being still, he could presently hear a murmuring from the bedroom window over his head. The gardener took from a tree a ladder that he had used in nailing that day, set it under the window, and ascended half-way, hoodwinking his conscience by seizing a nail or two with his hand and testing their twig-supporting powers. He soon heard enough to satisfy him. The words of a church-service in the strange parson's voice were audible in snatches through the blind: they were words he knew to be part of the solemnization of matrimony, such as 'wedded wife,' 'richer for poorer,' and so on; the less familiar parts being a more or less confused sound.

Satisfied that a wedding was in progress there, the gardener did not for a moment dream that one of the contracting parties could be other than the sick Baron. He descended the ladder and again walked round the house, waiting only till he saw Margery emerge from the same little door; when, fearing that he might be discovered, he withdrew in the direction of his own cottage.

This building stood at the lower corner of the garden, and as soon as the gardener entered he was accosted by a handsome woman in a widow's cap, who called him father, and said that supper had been ready for a long time. They sat down, but during the meal the gardener was so abstracted and silent that his daughter put her head winningly to one side and said, 'What is it, father dear?'

'Ah—what is it!' cried the gardener. 'Something that makes very little difference to me, but may be of great account to you, if you play your cards well. *There's been a wedding at the Lodge to-night!*' He related to her, with a caution to secrecy, all that he had heard and seen.

'We are folk that have got to get their living,' he said, 'and such ones mustn't tell tales about their betters,—Lord forgive the mockery of the word!—but there's something to be made of it. She's a nice maid; so, Harriet, do you take the first chance you get for honouring her, before others know what has happened. Since this is done so privately it will be kept private for some time—till after his death, no question;—when I expect she'll take this house for herself; and blaze out as a widow-lady ten thousand pound strong. You being a widow, she may make you her company-keeper; and so you'll have a home by a little contriving.'

While this conversation progressed at the gardener's Margery was on her way out of the Baron's house. She was, indeed, married. But, as we know, she was not married to the Baron. The ceremony over she seemed but little discomposed, and expressed a wish to return alone as she had come. To this, of course, no objection could be offered under the terms of the agreement, and wishing Jim a frigid good-bye, and the Baron a very quiet farewell, she went out by the door which had admitted her. Once safe and alone in the darkness of the park she burst into tears, which dropped upon the grass as she passed along. In the Baron's room she had seemed scared and helpless; now her reason and

53

emotions returned. The further she got away from the glamour of that room, and the influence of its occupant, the more she became of opinion that she had acted foolishly. She had disobediently left her father's house, to obey him here. She had pleased everybody but herself. However, thinking was now too late. How she got into her grandmother's house she hardly knew; but without a supper, and without confronting either her relative or Edy, she went to bed.

CHAPTER XIII.

On going out into the garden next morning, with a strange sense of being another person than herself, she beheld Jim leaning mutely over the gate. He nodded. 'Good morning, Margery,' he said civilly.

'Good morning,' said Margery in the same tone.

'I beg your pardon,' he continued. 'But which way was you going this morning?'

'I am not going anywhere just now, thank you. But I shall go to my father's by-and-by with Edy.' She went on with a sigh, 'I have done what he has all along wished, that is, married you; and there's no longer reason for enmity atween him and me.'

'Trew—trew. Well, as I am going the same way, I can give you a lift in the trap, for the distance is long.'

'No thank you—I am used to walking,' she said.

They remained in silence, the gate between them, till Jim's convictions would apparently allow him to hold his peace no longer. 'This is a bad job!' he murmured.

'It is,' she said, as one whose thoughts have only too readily been identified. 'How I came to agree to it is more than I can tell!' And tears began rolling down her cheeks.

'The blame is more mine than yours, I suppose,' he returned. 'I ought to have said No, and not backed up the gentleman in carrying out this scheme. 'Twas his own notion entirely, as perhaps you know. I should never have thought of such a plan; but he said you'd be willing, and that it would be all right; and I was too ready to believe him.'

'The thing is, how to remedy it,' said she bitterly. 'I believe, of course, in your promise to keep this private, and not to trouble me by calling.'

'Certainly,' said Jim. 'I don't want to trouble you. As for that, why, my dear Mrs. Hayward—'

'Don't Mrs. Hayward me!' said Margery sharply. 'I won't be Mrs. Hayward!'

Jim paused. 'Well, you are she by law, and that was all I meant,' he said mildly.

'I said I would acknowledge no such thing, and I won't. A thing can't be legal when it's against the wishes of the persons the laws are made to protect. So I beg you not to call me that anymore.'

'Very well, Miss Tucker,' said Jim deferentially. 'We can live on exactly as before. We can't marry anybody else, that's true; but beyond that there's no difference, and no harm done. Your father ought to be told, I suppose, even if nobody else is? It will partly reconcile him to you, and make your life smoother.'

Instead of directly replying, Margery exclaimed in a low voice:

'O, it is a mistake—I didn't see it all, owing to not having time to reflect! I agreed, thinking that at least I should get reconciled to father by the step. But perhaps he would as soon have me not married at all as married and parted. I must ha' been enchanted—bewitched—when I gave my consent to this! I only did it to please that dear good dying nobleman—though why he should have wished it so much I can't tell!'

'Nor I neither,' said Jim. 'Yes, we've been fooled into it, Margery,' he said, with extraordinary gravity. 'He's had his way wi' us, and now we've got to suffer for it. Being a gentleman of patronage, and having bought several loads of lime o' me, and having given me all that splendid furniture, I could hardly refuse—'

'What, did he give you that?'

'Ay sure—to help me win ye.'

Margery covered her face with her hands; whereupon Jim stood up from the gate and looked critically at her. ''Tis a footy plot between you two men to—snare me!' she exclaimed. 'Why should you have done it—why should he have done it—when I've not deserved to be treated so. He bought the furniture—did he! O, I've been taken in—I've been wronged!' The grief and vexation of finding that long ago, when fondly believing the Baron to have lover-like feelings himself for her, he was still conspiring to favour Jim's suit, was more than she could endure.

Jim with distant courtesy waited, nibbling a straw, till her paroxysm was over. 'One word, Miss Tuck—Mrs.—Margery,' he then recommenced gravely. 'You'll find me man enough to respect your wish, and to leave you to yourself—for ever and ever, if that's all. But I've just one word of advice to render 'ee. That is, that before you go to Silverthorn Dairy yourself you let me drive ahead and call on your father. He's friends with me, and he's not friends with you. I can break the news, a little at a time, and I think I can gain his good will for you now, even though the wedding be no natural wedding at all. At any count, I can hear what he's got to say about 'ee, and come back here and tell 'ee.'

She nodded a cool assent to this, and he left her strolling about the garden in the sunlight while he went on to reconnoitre as agreed. It must not be supposed that Jim's dutiful echoes of Margery's regret at her precipitate marriage were all gospel; and there is no doubt that his private intention, after telling the dairy-farmer what had happened, was to ask his temporary assent to her caprice, till, in the course of time, she should be reasoned out of her whims and induced to settle down with Jim in a natural manner. He had, it is true, been somewhat nettled by her firm objection to him, and her keen sorrow for what she had done to please another; but he hoped for the best.

But, alas for the astute Jim's calculations! He drove on to the dairy, whose white walls now gleamed in the morning sun; made fast the horse to a ring in the wall, and entered the barton. Before knocking, he perceived the dairyman walking across from a gate in the other direction, as if he had just come in. Jim went over to him. Since the unfortunate incident on the morning of the intended wedding they had merely been on nodding terms, from a sense of awkwardness in their relations.

'What—is that thee?' said Dairyman Tucker, in a voice which unmistakably startled Jim by its abrupt fierceness. 'A pretty fellow thou be'st!'

It was a bad beginning for the young man's life as a son-in-law, and augured ill for the delicate consultation he desired.

'What's the matter?' said Jim.

'Matter! I wish some folks would burn their lime without burning other folks' property along wi' it. You ought to be ashamed of yourself. You call yourself a man, Jim Hayward, and an honest lime-burner, and a respectable, market-keeping Christen, and yet at six o'clock this morning, instead o' being where you ought to ha' been—at your work, there was neither vell or mark o' thee to be seen!'

'Faith, I don't know what you are raving at,' said Jim.

'Why—the sparks from thy couch-heap blew over upon my hay-rick, and the rick's burnt to ashes; and all to come out o' my well-squeezed pocket. I'll tell thee what it is, young man. There's no business in thee. I've known Silverthorn folk, quick and dead, for the last couple-o'-score year, and I've never knew one so three-cunning for harm as thee, my gentleman lime-burner; and I reckon it one o' the luckiest days o' my life when I 'scaped having thee in my family. That maid of mine was right; I was wrong. She seed thee to be a drawlacheting rogue, and 'twas her wisdom to go off that morning and get rid o' thee. I commend her for' t, and I'm going to fetch her home to-morrow.'

'You needn't take the trouble. She's coming home-along to-night of her own accord. I have seen her this morning, and she told me so.'

'So much the better. I'll welcome her warm. Nation! I'd sooner see her married to the parish fool than thee. Not you—you don't care for my hay. Tarrying about where you shouldn't be, in bed, no doubt; that's what you was a-doing. Now, don't you darken my doors again, and the sooner you be off my bit o' ground the better I shall be pleased.'

Jim looked, as he felt, stultified. If the rick had been really destroyed, a little blame certainly attached to him, but he could not understand how it had happened. However, blame or none, it was clear he could not, with any self-respect, declare himself to be this peppery old gaffer's son-in-law in the face of such an attack as this.

For months—almost years—the one transaction that had seemed necessary to compose these two families satisfactorily was Jim's union with Margery. No sooner had it been completed than it appeared on all sides as the gravest mishap for both. Stating coldly that he would discover how much of the accident was to be attributed to his negligence, and pay the damage, he went out of the barton, and returned the way he had come.

Margery had been keeping a look-out for him, particularly wishing him not to enter the house, lest others should see the seriousness of their interview; and as soon as she heard wheels she went to the gate, which was out of view.

'Surely father has been speaking roughly to you!' she said, on seeing his face.

'Not the least doubt that he have,' said Jim.

'But is he still angry with me?'

'Not in the least. He's waiting to welcome 'ee.'

'Ah! because I've married you.'

'Because he thinks you have not married me! He's jawed me up hill and down. He hates me; and for your sake I have not explained a word.'

Margery looked towards home with a sad, severe gaze. 'Mr. Hayward,' she said, 'we have made a great mistake, and we are in a strange position.'

'True, but I'll tell you what, mistress—I won't stand—' He stopped suddenly. 'Well, well; I've promised!' he quietly added.

'We must suffer for our mistake,' she went on. 'The way to suffer least is to keep our own counsel on what happened last evening, and not to meet. I must now return to my father.'

He inclined his head in indifferent assent, and she went indoors, leaving him there.

CHAPTER XIV.

Margery returned home, as she had decided, and resumed her old life at Silverthorn. And seeing her father's animosity towards Jim, she told him not a word of the marriage.

Her inner life, however, was not what it once had been. She had suffered a mental and emotional displacement—a shock, which had set a shade of astonishment on her face as a permanent thing.

Her indignation with the Baron for collusion with Jim, at first bitter, lessened with the lapse of a few weeks, and at length vanished in the interest of some tidings she received one day.

The Baron was not dead, but he was no longer at the Lodge. To the surprise of the physicians, a sufficient improvement had taken place in his condition to permit of his removal before the cold weather came. His desire for removal had been such, indeed, that it was advisable to carry it out at almost any risk. The plan adopted had been to have him borne on men's shoulders in a sort of palanquin to the shore near Idmouth, a distance of several miles, where a yacht lay awaiting him. By this means the noise and jolting of a carriage, along irregular bye-roads, were avoided. The singular procession over the fields took place at night, and was witnessed by but few people, one being a labouring man, who described the scene to Margery. When the seaside was reached a long, narrow gangway was laid from the deck of the yacht to the shore, which was so steep as to allow the yacht to lie quite near. The men, with their burden, ascended by the light of lanterns, the sick man was laid in the cabin, and, as soon as his bearers had returned to the shore, the gangway was removed, a rope was heard skirring over wood in the darkness, the yacht quivered, spread her woven wings to the air, and moved away. Soon she was but a small, shapeless phantom upon the wide breast of the sea.

It was said that the yacht was bound for Algiers.

When the inimical autumn and winter weather came on, Margery wondered if he were still alive. The house being shut up, and the servants gone, she had no means of knowing, till, on a particular Saturday, her father drove her to Exonbury market. Here, in attending to his business, he left her to herself for awhile. Walking in a quiet street in the professional quarter of the town, she saw coming towards her the solicitor who had been present at the wedding, and who had acted for the Baron in various small local matters during his brief residence at the Lodge.

She reddened to peony hues, averted her eyes, and would have passed him. But he crossed over and barred the pavement, and when she met his glance he was looking with friendly severity at her. The street was quiet, and he said in a low voice, 'How's the husband?'

'I don't know, sir,' said she.

'What—and are your stipulations about secrecy and separate living still in force?'

'They will always be,' she replied decisively. 'Mr. Hayward and I agreed on the point, and we have not the slightest wish to change the arrangement.'

'H'm. Then 'tis Miss Tucker to the world; Mrs. Hayward to me and one or two others only?'

Margery nodded. Then she nerved herself by an effort, and, though blushing painfully, asked, 'May I put one question, sir? Is the Baron dead?'

'He is dead to you and to all of us. Why should you ask?'

'Because, if he's alive, I am sorry I married James Hayward. If he is dead I do not much mind my marriage.'

'I repeat, he is dead to you,' said the lawyer emphatically. 'I'll tell you all I know. My professional services for him ended with his departure from this country; but I think I should have heard from him if he had been alive still. I have not heard at all: and this, taken in connection with the nature of his illness, leaves no doubt in my mind that he is dead.'

Margery sighed, and thanking the lawyer she left him with a tear for the Baron in her eye. After this incident she became more restful; and the time drew on for her periodical visit to her grandmother.

A few days subsequent to her arrival her aged relative asked her to go with a message to the gardener at Mount Lodge (who still lived on there, keeping the grounds in order for the landlord). Margery hated that direction now, but she went. The Lodge, which she saw over the trees, was to her like a skull from which the warm and living flesh had vanished. It was twilight by the time she reached the cottage at the bottom of the Lodge garden, and, the room being illuminated within, she saw through the window a woman she had never seen before. She was dark, and rather handsome, and when Margery knocked she opened the door. It was the gardener' s widowed daughter, who had been advised to make friends with Margery.

She now found her opportunity. Margery' s errand was soon completed, the young widow, to her surprise, treating her with preternatural respect, and afterwards offering to accompany her home. Margery was not sorry to have a companion in the gloom, and they walked on together. The widow, Mrs. Peach, was demonstrative and confidential; and told Margery all about herself. She had come quite recently to live with her father—during the Baron' s illness, in fact—and her husband had been captain of a ketch.

'I saw you one morning, ma' am,' she said. 'But you didn' t see me. It was when you were crossing the hill in sight of the Lodge. You looked at it, and sighed. ' Tis the lot of widows to sigh, ma' am, is it not?'

'Widows—yes, I suppose; but what do you mean?'

Mrs. Peach lowered her voice. 'I can' t say more, ma' am, with proper respect. But there seems to be no question of the poor Baron' s death; and though these foreign princes can take (as my poor husband used to tell me) what they call left-handed wives, and leave them behind when they go abroad, widowhood is widowhood, left-handed or right. And really, to be the left-handed wife of a foreign baron is nobler than to be married all round to a common man. You' ll excuse my freedom, ma' am; but being a widow myself, I have pitied you from my heart; so young as you are, and having to keep it a secret, and (excusing me) having no money out of his vast riches because ' tis swallowed up by Baroness Number One.'

Now Margery did not understand a word more of this than the bare fact that Mrs. Peach suspected her to be the Baron' s undowered widow, and such was the milkmaid' s nature that she did not deny the widow' s impeachment. The latter continued—

'But ah, ma' am, all your troubles are straight backward in your memory—while I have troubles before as well as grief behind.'

'What may they be, Mrs. Peach?' inquired Margery with an air of the Baroness.

The other dropped her voice to revelation tones: 'I have been forgetful enough of my first man to lose my heart to a second!'

'You shouldn' t do that—it is wrong. You should control your feelings.'

'But how am I to control my feelings?'

'By going to your dead husband' s grave, and things of that sort.'

'Do you go to your dead husband' s grave?'

'How can I go to Algiers?'

'Ah—too true! Well, I' ve tried everything to cure myself—read the words against it, gone to the Table the first Sunday of every month, and all sorts. But, avast, my shipmate!—as my poor man used to say—there ' tis just the same. In short, I' ve made up my mind to encourage the new one. ' Tis flattering that I, a new-comer, should have been found out by a young man so soon.'

'Who is he?' said Margery listlessly.

'A master lime-burner.'

'A master lime-burner?'

'That' s his profession. He' s a partner-in-co., doing very well indeed.'

'But what' s his name?'

'I don' t like to tell you his name, for, though ' tis night, that covers all shame-facedness, my face is as hot as a ' Talian iron, I declare! Do you just feel it.'

Margery put her hand on Mrs. Peach' s face, and, sure enough, hot it was. 'Does he come courting?' she asked quickly.

'Well only in the way of business. He never comes unless lime is wanted in the neighbourhood. He' s in the Yeomanry, too, and will look very fine when he comes out in regimentals for drill in May.'

'Oh—in the Yeomanry,' Margery said, with a slight relief. 'Then it can' t—is he a young man?'

'Yes, junior partner-in-co.'

The description had an odd resemblance to Jim, of whom Margery had not heard a word for months. He had promised silence and absence, and had fulfilled his promise literally, with a gratuitous addition that was rather amazing, if indeed it were Jim whom the widow loved. One point in the description puzzled Margery: Jim was not in the Yeomanry, unless, by a surprising development of enterprise, he had entered it recently.

At parting Margery said, with an interest quite tender, 'I should like to see you again, Mrs. Peach, and hear of your attachment. When can you call?'

'Oh—any time, dear Baroness, I'm sure—if you think I am good enough.'

'Indeed, I do, Mrs. Peach. Come as soon as you've seen the lime-burner again.'

CHAPTER XV.

Seeing that Jim lived several miles from the widow, Margery was rather surprised, and even felt a slight sinking of the heart, when her new acquaintance appeared at her door so soon as the evening of the following Monday. She asked Margery to walk out with her, which the young woman readily did.

'I am come at once,' said the widow breathlessly, as soon as they were in the lane, 'for it is so exciting that I can't keep it. I must tell it to somebody, if only a bird, or a cat, or a garden snail.'

'What is it?' asked her companion.

'I've pulled grass from my husband's grave to cure it—wove the blades into true lover's knots; took off my shoes upon the sod; but, avast, my shipmate,—'

'Upon the sod—why?'

'To feel the damp earth he's in, and make the sense of it enter my soul. But no. It has swelled to a head; he is going to meet me at the Yeomanry Review.'

'The master lime-burner?'
The widow nodded.

'When is it to be?'

'To-morrow. He looks so lovely in his accoutrements! He's such a splendid soldier; that was the last straw that kindled my soul to say yes. He's home from Exonbury for a night between the drills,' continued Mrs. Peach. 'He goes back to-morrow morning for the Review, and when it's over he's going to meet me. But, guide my heart, there he is!'

Her exclamation had rise in the sudden appearance of a brilliant red uniform through the trees, and the tramp of a horse carrying the wearer thereof. In another half-minute the military gentleman would have turned the corner, and faced them.

'He'd better not see me; he'll think I know too much,' said Margery precipitately. 'I'll go up here.'
The widow, whose thoughts had been of the same cast, seemed much

62

relieved to see Margery disappear in the plantation, in the midst of a spring chorus of birds. Once among the trees, Margery turned her head, and, before she could see the rider's person she recognized the horse as Tony, the lightest of three that Jim and his partner owned, for the purpose of carting out lime to their customers.

Jim, then, had joined the Yeomanry since his estrangement from Margery. A man who had worn the young Queen Victoria's uniform for seven days only could not be expected to look as if it were part of his person, in the manner of long-trained soldiers; but he was a well-formed young fellow, and of an age when few positions came amiss to one who has the capacity to adapt himself to circumstances.

Meeting the blushing Mrs. Peach (to whom Margery in her mind sternly denied the right to blush at all), Jim alighted and moved on with her, probably at Mrs. Peach's own suggestion; so that what they said, how long they remained together, and how they parted, Margery knew not. She might have known some of these things by waiting; but the presence of Jim had bred in her heart a sudden disgust for the widow, and a general sense of discomfiture. She went away in an opposite direction, turning her head and saying to the unconscious Jim, 'There's a fine rod in pickle for you, my gentleman, if you carry out that pretty scheme!'

Jim's military *coup* had decidedly astonished her. What he might do next she could not conjecture. The idea of his doing anything sufficiently brilliant to arrest her attention would have seemed ludicrous, had not Jim, by entering the Yeomanry, revealed a capacity for dazzling exploits which made it unsafe to predict any limitation to his powers. Margery was now excited. The daring of the wretched Jim in bursting into scarlet amazed her as much as his doubtful acquaintanceship with the demonstrative Mrs. Peach. To go to that Review, to watch the pair, to eclipse Mrs. Peach in brilliancy, to meet and pass them in withering contempt—if she only could do it! But, alas! she was a forsaken woman.

'If the Baron were alive, or in England,' she said to herself (for sometimes she thought he might possibly be alive), 'and he were to take me to this Review, wouldn't I show that forward Mrs. Peach what a lady is like, and keep among the select company, and not mix with the common people at all!'

It might at first sight be thought that the best course for Margery at this juncture would have been to go to Jim, and nip the intrigue in the bud without further scruple. But her own declaration in after days was that whoever could say that was far from realizing her situation. It was hard to break such ice as divided their two lives now, and to attempt it at that moment was a too humiliating proclamation of defeat. The only plan she could think of—perhaps not a wise one in the circumstances—was to go to the Review herself; and be the gayest there.

A method of doing this with some propriety soon occurred to her. She dared not ask her father, who scorned to waste time in sight-seeing, and whose animosity towards Jim knew no abatement; but she might call on her old acquaintance, Mr. Vine, Jim's partner, who would probably be going with the rest of the holiday-folk, and ask if she might accompany him in his spring-trap. She had no sooner perceived the feasibility of this, through her being at her grandmother's, than she decided to meet with the old man early the next morning.

In the meantime Jim and Mrs. Peach had walked slowly along the road together, Jim leading the horse, and Mrs. Peach informing him that her father, the gardener, was at Jim's village further on, and that she had come to meet him. Jim, for reasons of his own, was going to sleep at his partner's that night, and thus their route was the same. The shades of eve closed in upon them as they walked, and by the time they reached the lime-kiln, which it was necessary to pass to get to the village, it was quite dark. Jim stopped at the kiln, to see if matters had progressed rightly in his seven days' absence, and Mrs. Peach, who stuck to him like a teazle, stopped also, saying she would wait for her father there. She held the horse while he ascended to the top of the kiln. Then rejoining her, and not quite knowing what to do, he stood beside her looking at the flames, which to-night burnt up brightly, shining a long way into the dark air, even up to the ramparts of the earthwork above them, and overhead into the bosoms of the clouds.

It was during this proceeding that a carriage, drawn by a pair of dark horses, came along the turnpike road. The light of the kiln caused the horses to swerve a little, and the occupant of the carriage looked out. He saw the bluish, lightning-like flames from the limestone, rising from the top of the furnace, and hard by the figures of Jim Hayward, the widow, and the horse, standing out with spectral distinctness against the mass of night behind. The scene wore the aspect of some unholy assignation in Pandaemonium, and it was all the more impressive from the fact that both Jim and the woman were quite unconscious of the striking spectacle they presented. The gentleman in the carriage watched them till he was borne out of sight.

Having seen to the kiln, Jim and the widow walked on again, and soon Mrs. Peach's father met them, and relieved Jim of the lady. When they had parted, Jim, with an expiration not unlike a breath of relief; went on to Mr. Vine's, and, having put the horse into the stable, entered the house. His partner was seated at the table, solacing himself after the labours of the day by luxurious alternations between a long clay pipe and a mug of perry.

'Well,' said Jim eagerly, 'what' s the news—how do she take it?'

'Sit down—sit down,' said Vine. '' Tis working well; not but that I deserve something o' thee for the trouble I' ve had in watching her. The soldiering was a fine move; but the woman is a better!—who invented it?'

'I myself,' said Jim modestly.

'Well; jealousy is making her rise like a thunderstorm, and in a day or two you' ll have her for the asking, my sonny. What' s the next step?'

'The widow is getting rather a weight upon a feller, worse luck,' said Jim. 'But I must keep it up until to-morrow, at any rate. I have promised to see her at the Review, and now the great thing is that Margery should see we a-smiling together—I in my full-dress uniform and clinking arms o' war. ' Twill be a good strong sting, and will end the business, I hope. Couldn' t you manage to put the hoss in and drive her there? She' d go if you were to ask her.'

'With all my heart,' said Mr. Vine, moistening the end of a new pipe in his perry. 'I can call at her grammer' s for her—' twill be all in my way.'

CHAPTER XVI.

Margery duly followed up her intention by arraying herself the next morning in her loveliest guise, and keeping watch for Mr. Vine' s appearance upon the high road, feeling certain that his would form one in the procession of carts and carriages which set in towards Exonbury that day. Jim had gone by at a very early hour, and she did not see him pass. Her anticipation was verified by the advent of Mr. Vine about eleven o' clock, dressed to his highest effort; but Margery was surprised to find that, instead of her having to stop him, he pulled in towards the gate of his own accord. The invitation planned between Jim and the old man on the previous night was now promptly given, and, as may be supposed, as promptly accepted. Such a strange coincidence she had never before known. She was quite ready, and they drove onward at once.

The Review was held on some high ground a little way out of the city, and her conductor suggested that they should put up the horse at the inn, and walk to the field—a plan which pleased her well, for it was more easy to take preliminary observations on foot without being seen herself than when sitting elevated in a vehicle.

They were just in time to secure a good place near the front, and in a few minutes after their arrival the reviewing officer came on the ground. Margery's eye had rapidly run over the troop in which Jim was enrolled, and she discerned him in one of the ranks, looking remarkably new and bright, both as to uniform and countenance. Indeed, if she had not worked herself into such a desperate state of mind she would have felt proud of him then and there. His shapely upright figure was quite noteworthy in the row of rotund yeomen on his right and left; while his charger Tony expressed by his bearing, even more than Jim, that he knew nothing about lime-carts whatever, and everything about trumpets and glory. How Jim could have scrubbed Tony to such shining blackness she could not tell, for the horse in his natural state was ingrained with lime-dust, that burnt the colour out of his coat as it did out of Jim's hair. Now he pranced martially, and was a war-horse every inch of him.

Having discovered Jim her next search was for Mrs. Peach, and, by dint of some oblique glancing Margery indignantly discovered the widow in the most forward place of all, her head and bright face conspicuously advanced; and, what was more shocking, she had abandoned her mourning for a violet drawn-bonnet and a gay spencer, together with a parasol luxuriously fringed in a way Margery had never before seen.

'Where did she get the money?' said Margery, under her breath.

'And to forget that poor sailor so soon!'

These general reflections were precipitately postponed by her discovering that Jim and the widow were perfectly alive to each other's whereabouts, and in the interchange of telegraphic signs of affection, which on the latter's part took the form of a playful fluttering of her handkerchief or waving of her parasol. Richard Vine had placed Margery in front of him, to protect her from the crowd, as he said, he himself surveying the scene over her bonnet. Margery would have been even more surprised than she was if she had known that Jim was not only aware of Mrs. Peach's presence, but also of her own, the treacherous Mr. Vine having drawn out his flame-coloured handkerchief and waved it to Jim over the young woman's head as soon as they had taken up their position.

'My partner makes a tidy soldier, eh—Miss Tucker?' said the senior lime-burner. 'It is my belief as a Christian that he's got a party here that he's making signs to—that handsome figure o' fun straight over-right him.'

'Perhaps so,' she said.

'And it's growing warm between 'em if I don't mistake,' continued the merciless Vine.

Margery was silent, biting her lip; and the troops being now set in motion, all signalling ceased for the present between soldier Hayward and his pretended sweetheart.

'Have you a piece of paper that I could make a memorandum on, Mr. Vine?' asked Margery.

Vine took out his pocket-book and tore a leaf from it, which he handed her with a pencil.

'Don't move from here—I'll return in a minute,' she continued, with the innocence of a woman who means mischief. And, withdrawing herself to the back, where the grass was clear, she pencilled down the words

'JIM'S MARRIED.'

Armed with this document she crept into the throng behind the unsuspecting Mrs. Peach, slipped the paper into her pocket on the top of her handkerchief; and withdrew unobserved, rejoining Mr. Vine with a bearing of *nonchalance*.

By-and-by the troops were in different order, Jim taking a left-hand position almost close to Mrs. Peach. He bent down and said a few words to her. From her manner of nodding assent it was surely some arrangement about a meeting by-and-by when Jim's drill was over, and Margery was more certain of the fact when, the Review having ended, and the people having strolled off to another part of the field where sports were to take place, Mrs. Peach tripped away in the direction of the city.

'I'll just say a word to my partner afore he goes off the ground, if you'll spare me a minute,' said the old lime-burner. 'Please stay here till I'm back again.' He edged along the front till he reached Jim.

'How is she?' said the latter.

'In a trimming sweat,' said Mr. Vine. 'And my counsel to 'ee is to carry this larry no further. 'Twill do no good. She's as ready to make friends with 'ee as any wife can be; and more showing off can only do harm.'

'But I must finish off with a spurt,' said Jim. 'And this is how I am going to do it. I have arranged with Mrs. Peach that, as soon as we soldiers have entered the town and been dismissed, I'll meet her there. It is really to say good-bye, but she don't know that; and I wanted it to look like a lopement to Margery's eyes. When I'm clear of Mrs. Peach I'll come back here and make it up with Margery on the spot.

67

But don't say I'm coming, or she may be inclined to throw off again. Just hint to her that I may be meaning to be off to London with the widow.'

The old man still insisted that this was going too far.

'No, no, it isn't,' said Jim. 'I know how to manage her. 'Twill just mellow her heart nicely by the time I come back. I must bring her down real tender, or 'twill all fail.'

His senior reluctantly gave in and returned to Margery. A short time afterwards the Yeomanry band struck up, and Jim with the regiment followed towards Exonbury.

'Yes, yes; they are going to meet,' said Margery to herself, perceiving that Mrs. Peach had so timed her departure as to be in the town at Jim's dismounting.

'Now we will go and see the games,' said Mr. Vine; 'they are really worth seeing. There's greasy poles, and jumping in sacks, and other trials of the intellect, that nobody ought to miss who wants to be abreast of his generation.'

Margery felt so indignant at the apparent assignation, which seemed about to take place despite her anonymous writing, that she helplessly assented to go anywhere, dropping behind Vine, that he might not see her mood.

Jim followed out his programme with literal exactness. No sooner was the troop dismissed in the city than he sent Tony to stable and joined Mrs. Peach, who stood on the edge of the pavement expecting him. But this acquaintance was to end: he meant to part from her for ever and in the quickest time, though civilly; for it was important to be with Margery as soon as possible. He had nearly completed the manœuvre to his satisfaction when, in drawing her handkerchief from her pocket to wipe the tears from her eyes, Mrs. Peach's hand grasped the paper, which she read at once.

'What! is that true?' she said, holding it out to Jim.

Jim started and admitted that it was, beginning an elaborate explanation and apologies. But Mrs. Peach was thoroughly roused, and then overcome. 'He's married, he's married!' she said, and swooned, or feigned to swoon, so that Jim was obliged to support her.

'He's married, he's married!' said a boy hard by who watched the scene with interest.

'He's married, he's married!' said a hilarious group of other boys near, with smiles several inches broad, and shining teeth; and so the exclamation echoed down the street.

Jim cursed his ill-luck; the loss of time that this dilemma entailed grew serious; for Mrs. Peach was now in such a hysterical state that he could not leave her with any good grace or feeling. It was necessary to take her to a refreshment room, lavish restoratives upon her, and altogether to waste nearly half an hour. When she had kept him as long as she chose, she forgave him; and thus at last he got away, his heart swelling with tenderness towards Margery. He at once hurried up the street to effect the reconciliation with her.

'How shall I do it?' he said to himself. 'Why, I'll step round to her side, fish for her hand, draw it through my arm as if I wasn't aware of it. Then she'll look in my face, I shall look in hers, and we shall march off the field triumphant, and the thing will be done without takings or tears.'

He entered the field and went straight as an arrow to the place appointed for the meeting. It was at the back of a refreshment tent outside the mass of spectators, and divided from their view by the tent itself. He turned the corner of the canvas, and there beheld Vine at the indicated spot. But Margery was not with him.

Vine's hat was thrust back into his poll. His face was pale, and his manner bewildered. 'Hullo? what's the matter?' said Jim.

'Where's my Margery?'

'You've carried this footy game too far, my man!' exclaimed Vine, with the air of a friend who has 'always told you so.' 'You ought to have dropped it several days ago, when she would have come to 'ee like a cooing dove. Now this is the end o' t!'

'Hey! what, my Margery? Has anything happened, for God's sake?'

'She's gone.'

'Where to?'

'That's more than earthly man can tell! I never see such a thing! 'Twas a stroke o' the black art—as if she were sperrited away. When we got to the games I said—mind, you told me to!—I said, "Jim Hayward thinks o' going off to London with that widow woman" — mind you told me to! She showed no wonderment, though a' seemed very low. Then she said to me, "I don't like standing here in this slummocky crowd. I shall feel more at home among the gentlepeople." And then she went to where the carriages were drawn up, and near her there was a grand coach, a-blazing with lions and unicorns, and hauled by two coal-black horses. I hardly thought much of it then, and by degrees lost sight of her behind it. Presently the other carriages moved off, and I thought still to see her standing there. But no, she had vanished; and then I saw the grand coach rolling away, and glimpsed Margery in it, beside a fine dark gentleman with black mustachios, and a very pale prince-like face. As soon as the horses got into the hard road they rattled on like hell-and-skimmer, and went out of sight in the dust, and—that's all. If you'd come back a little sooner you'd ha' caught her.'

Jim had turned whiter than his pipeclay. 'O, this is too bad—too bad!' he cried in anguish, striking his brow. 'That paper and that fainting woman kept me so long. Who could have done it? But 'tis my fault. I've stung her too much. I shouldn't have carried it so far.'

'You shouldn't—just what I said,' replied his senior.

'She thinks I've gone off with that cust widow; and to spite me she's gone off with the man! Do you know who that stranger wi' the lions and unicorns is? Why, 'tis that foreigner who calls himself a Baron, and took Mount Lodge for six months last year to make mischief—a villain! O, my Margery—that it should come to this! She's lost, she's ruined!—Which way did they go?'

Jim turned to follow in the direction indicated, when, behold, there stood at his back her father, Dairyman Tucker.

'Now look here, young man,' said Dairyman Tucker. 'I've just heard all that wailing—and straightway will ask 'ee to stop it sharp. 'Tis like your brazen impudence to teave and wail when you be another woman's husband; yes, faith, I see'd her a-fainting in yer arms when you wanted to get away from her, and honest folk a-standing round who knew you'd married her, and said so. I heard it, though you didn't see me. "He's married!" says they. Some sly register-office business, no doubt; but sly doings will out. As for Margery—who's to be called higher titles in these parts hencefor'ard—I'm her father, and I say it's all right what she's done. Don't I know private news, hey? Haven't I just learnt that secret weddings of high people can happen at expected deathbeds by special licence, as well as low people at registrars' offices? And can't husbands come back and claim their own when they choose? Begone, young man, and leave noblemen's wives alone; and I thank God I shall be rid of a numskull!'

Swift words of explanation rose to Jim's lips, but they paused there and died. At that last moment he could not, as Margery's husband, announce Margery's shame and his own, and transform her father's triumph to wretchedness at a blow.

'I—I—must leave here,' he stammered. Going from the place in an opposite course to that of the fugitives, he doubled when out of sight, and in an incredibly short space had entered the town. Here he made inquiries for the emblazoned carriage, and gained from one or two persons a general idea of its route. They thought it had taken the highway to London. Saddling poor Tony before he had half eaten his corn, Jim galloped along the same road.

CHAPTER XVII.

Now Jim was quite mistaken in supposing that by leaving the field in a roundabout manner he had deceived Dairyman Tucker as to his object. That astute old man immediately divined that Jim was meaning to track the fugitives, in ignorance (as the dairyman supposed) of their lawful relation. He was soon assured of the fact, for, creeping to a remote angle of the field, he saw Jim hastening into the town. Vowing vengeance on the young lime-burner for his mischievous interference between a nobleman and his secretly-wedded wife, the dairy-farmer determined to balk him.

Tucker had ridden on to the Review ground, so that there was no necessity for him, as there had been for poor Jim, to re-enter the town before starting. The dairyman hastily untied his mare from the row of other horses, mounted, and descended to a bridle-path which would take him obliquely into the London road a mile or so ahead. The old man's route being along one side of an equilateral triangle, while Jim's was along two sides of the same, the former was at the point of intersection long before Hayward.

Arrived here, the dairyman pulled up and looked around. It was a spot at which the highway forked; the left arm, the more important, led on through Sherton Abbas and Melchester to London; the right to Idmouth and the coast. Nothing was visible on the white track to London; but on the other there appeared the back of a carriage, which rapidly ascended a distant hill and vanished under the trees. It was the Baron's who, according to the sworn information of the gardener at Mount Lodge, had made Margery his wife.

The carriage having vanished, the dairyman gazed in the opposite direction, towards Exonbury. Here he beheld Jim in his regimentals, laboriously approaching on Tony's back.

Soon he reached the forking roads, and saw the dairyman by the wayside. But Jim did not halt. Then the dairyman practised the greatest duplicity of his life.

71

'Right along the London road, if you want to catch ' em!' he said.

'Thank ' ee, dairyman, thank ' ee!' cried Jim, his pale face lighting up with gratitude, for he believed that Tucker had learnt his mistake from Vine, and had come to his assistance. Without drawing rein he diminished along the road not taken by the flying pair. The dairyman rubbed his hands with delight, and returned to the city as the cathedral clock struck five.

Jim pursued his way through the dust, up hill and down hill; but never saw ahead of him the vehicle of his search. That vehicle was passing along a diverging way at a distance of many miles from where he rode. Still he sped onwards, till Tony showed signs of breaking down; and then Jim gathered from inquiries he made that he had come the wrong way. It burst upon his mind that the dairyman, still ignorant of the truth, had misinformed him. Heavier in his heart than words can describe he turned Tony's drooping head, and resolved to drag his way home.

But the horse was now so jaded that it was impossible to proceed far. Having gone about half a mile back he came again to a small roadside hamlet and inn, where he put up Tony for a rest and feed. As for himself, there was no quiet in him. He tried to sit and eat in the inn kitchen; but he could not stay there. He went out, and paced up and down the road. Standing in sight of the white way by which he had come he beheld advancing towards him the horses and carriage he sought, now black and daemonic against the slanting fires of the western sun.

The why and wherefore of this sudden appearance he did not pause to consider. His resolve to intercept the carriage was instantaneous. He ran forward, and doggedly waiting barred the way to the advancing equipage. The Baron's coachman shouted, but Jim stood firm as a rock, and on the former attempting to push past him Jim drew his sword, resolving to cut the horses down rather than be displaced. The animals were thrown nearly back upon their haunches, and at this juncture a gentleman looked out of the window. It was the Baron himself.

'Who's there?' he inquired.

'James Hayward!' replied the young man fiercely, 'and he demands his wife.'

The Baron leapt out, and told the coachman to drive back out of sight and wait for him.

'I was hastening to find you,' he said to Jim. 'Your wife is where she ought to be, and where you ought to be also—by your own fireside. Where's the other woman?'

Jim, without replying, looked incredulously into the carriage as it turned. Margery was certainly not there. 'The other woman is nothing to me,' he said bitterly. 'I used her to warm up Margery: I have now done with her. The question I ask, my lord, is, what business had you with Margery to-day?'

'My business was to help her to regain the husband she had seemingly lost. I saw her; she told me you had eloped by the London road with another. I, who have—mostly—had her happiness at heart, told her I would help her to follow you if she wished. She gladly agreed; we drove after, but could hear no tidings of you in front of us. Then I took her—to your house—and there she awaits you. I promised to send you to her if human effort could do it, and was tracking you for that purpose.'

'Then you've been a-pursuing after me?'

'You and the widow.'

'And I've been pursuing after you and Margery! My noble lord, your actions seem to show that I ought to believe you in this; and when you say you've her happiness at heart, I don't forget that you've formerly proved it to be so. Well, Heaven forbid that I should think wrongfully of you if you don't deserve it! A mystery to me you have always been, my noble lord, and in this business more than in any.'

'I am glad to hear you say no worse. In one hour you'll have proof of my conduct—good and bad. Can I do anything more? Say the word, and I'll try.'

Jim reflected. 'Baron,' he said, 'I am a plain man, and wish only to lead a quiet life with my wife, as a man should. You have great power over her—power to any extent, for good or otherwise. If you command her anything on earth, righteous or questionable, that she'll do. So that, since you ask me if you can do more for me, I'll answer this, you can promise never to see her again. I mean no harm, my lord; but your presence can do no good; you will trouble us. If I return to her, will you for ever stay away?'

'Hayward,' said the Baron, 'I swear to you that I will disturb you and your wife by my presence no more. And he took Jim's hand, and pressed it within his own upon the hilt of Jim's sword.

In relating this incident to the present narrator Jim used to declare that, to his fancy, the ruddy light of the setting sun burned with more than earthly fire on the Baron's face as the words were spoken; and that the ruby flash of his eye in the same light was what he never witnessed before nor since in the eye of mortal man. After this there was nothing more to do or say in that place. Jim accompanied his never-to-be-forgotten acquaintance to the carriage, closed the door after him, waved his hat to him, and from that hour he and the Baron met not again on earth.

A few words will suffice to explain the fortunes of Margery while the foregoing events were in action elsewhere. On leaving her companion Vine she had gone distractedly among the carriages, the rather to escape his observation than of any set purpose. Standing here she thought she heard her name pronounced, and turning, saw her foreign friend, whom she had supposed to be, if not dead, a thousand miles off. He beckoned, and she went close. 'You are ill—you are wretched,' he said, looking keenly in her face. 'Where's your husband?'

She told him her sad suspicion that Jim had run away from her. The Baron reflected, and inquired a few other particulars of her late life. Then he said: 'You and I must find him. Come with me.' At this word of command from the Baron she had entered the carriage as docilely as a child, and there she sat beside him till he chose to speak, which was not till they were some way out of the town, at the forking ways, and the Baron had discovered that Jim was certainly not, as they had supposed, making off from Margery along that particular branch of the fork that led to London.

'To pursue him in this way is useless, I perceive,' he said. 'And the proper course now is that I should take you to his house. That done I will return, and bring him to you if mortal persuasion can do it.'

'I didn't want to go to his house without him, sir,' said she, tremblingly.

'Didn't want to!' he answered. 'Let me remind you, Margery Hayward, that your place is in your husband's house. Till you are there you have no right to criticize his conduct, however wild it may be. Why have you not been there before?'

'I don't know, sir,' she murmured, her tears falling silently upon her hand.

'Don't you think you ought to be there?'

She did not answer.

'Of course you ought.'

Still she did not speak.

The Baron sank into silence, and allowed his eye to rest on her. What thoughts were all at once engaging his mind after those moments of reproof? Margery had given herself into his hands without a remonstrance, her husband had apparently deserted her. She was absolutely in his power, and they were on the high road.

That his first impulse in inviting her to accompany him had been the legitimate one denoted by his words cannot reasonably be doubted. That his second was otherwise soon became revealed, though not at first to her, for she was too bewildered to notice where they were going. Instead of turning and taking the road to Jim's, the Baron, as if influenced suddenly by her reluctance to return thither if Jim was playing truant, signalled to the coachman to take the branch road to the right, as her father had discerned.

They soon approached the coast near Idmouth. The carriage stopped. Margery awoke from her reverie.

'Where are we?' she said, looking out of the window, with a start. Before her was an inlet of the sea, and in the middle of the inlet rode a yacht, its masts repeating as if from memory the rocking they had practised in their native forest.

'At a little sea-side nook, where my yacht lies at anchor,' he said tentatively. 'Now, Margery, in five minutes we can be aboard, and in half an hour we can be sailing away all the world over. Will you come?'

'I cannot decide,' she said, in low tones.

'Why not?'

'Because—'

Then on a sudden, Margery seemed to see all contingencies: she became white as a fleece, and a bewildered look came into her eyes. With clasped hands she leant on the Baron.

Baron von Xanten observed her distracted look, averted his face, and coming to a decision opened the carriage door, quickly mounted outside, and in a second or two the carriage left the shore behind, and ascended the road by which it had come.

In about an hour they reached Jim Hayward's home. The Baron alighted, and spoke to her through the window. 'Margery, can you forgive a lover's bad impulse, which I swear was unpremeditated?' he asked. 'If you can, shake my hand.'

She did not do it, but eventually allowed him to help her out of the carriage. He seemed to feel the awkwardness keenly; and seeing it, she said, 'Of course I forgive you, sir, for I felt for a moment as you did. Will you send my husband to me?'

'I will, if any man can,' said he. 'Such penance is milder than I deserve! God bless you and give you happiness! I shall never see you again!' He turned, entered the carriage, and was gone; and having found out Jim's course, came up with him upon the road as described. In due time the latter reached his lodging at his partner's. The woman who took care of the house in Vine's absence at once told Jim that a lady who had come in a carriage was waiting for him in his sitting-room. Jim proceeded thither with agitation, and beheld, shrinkingly ensconced in the large slippery chair, and surrounded by the brilliant articles that had so long awaited her, his long-estranged wife.

Margery's eyes were round and fear-stricken. She essayed to speak, but Jim, strangely enough, found the readier tongue then. 'Why did I do it, you would ask,' he said. 'I cannot tell. Do you forgive my deception? O Margery—you are my Margery still! But how could you trust yourself in the Baron's hands this afternoon, without knowing him better?'

'He said I was to come, and I went,' she said, as well as she could for tearfulness.

'You obeyed him blindly.'

'I did. But perhaps I was not justified in doing it.'

'I don't know,' said Jim musingly. 'I think he's a good man.' Margery did not explain. And then a sunnier mood succeeded her tremblings and tears, till old Mr. Vine came into the house below, and Jim went down to declare that all was well, and sent off his partner to break the news to Margery's father, who as yet remained unenlightened.

The dairyman bore the intelligence of his daughter's untitled state as best he could, and punished her by not coming near her for several weeks, though at last he grumbled his forgiveness, and made up matters with Jim. The handsome Mrs. Peach vanished to Plymouth, and found another sailor, not without a reasonable complaint against Jim and Margery both that she had been unfairly used.

As for the mysterious gentleman who had exercised such an influence over their lives, he kept his word, and was a stranger to Lower Wessex thenceforward. Baron or no Baron, Englishman or foreigner, he had shown a genuine interest in Jim, and real sorrow for a certain reckless phase of his acquaintance with Margery. That he had a more tender feeling toward the young girl than he wished her or any one else to perceive there could be no doubt. That he was strongly tempted at times to adopt other than conventional courses with regard to her is also clear, particularly at that critical hour when she rolled along the high road with him in the carriage, after turning from the fancied pursuit of Jim. But at other times he schooled impassioned sentiments into fair conduct, which even erred on the side of harshness. In after years there was a report that another attempt on his life with a pistol, during one of those fits of moodiness to which he seemed constitutionally liable, had been effectual; but nobody in Silverthorn was in a position to ascertain the truth.

There he is still regarded as one who had something about him magical and unearthly. In his mystery let him remain; for a man, no less than a landscape, who awakens an interest under uncertain lights and touches of unfathomable shade, may cut but a poor figure in a garish noontide shine. When she heard of his mournful death Margery sat in her nursing-chair, gravely thinking for nearly ten minutes, to the total neglect of her infant in the cradle. Jim, from the other side of the fire-place, said: 'You are sorry enough for him, Margery. I am sure of that.'

'Yes, yes,' she murmured, 'I am sorry.' After a moment she added: 'Now that he's dead I'll make a confession, Jim, that I have never made to a soul. If he had pressed me—which he did not—to go with him when I was in the carriage that night beside his yacht, I would have gone. And I was disappointed that he did not press me.'

'Suppose he were to suddenly appear now, and say in a voice of command, "Margery, come with me!"'

'I believe I should have no power to disobey,' she returned, with a mischievous look. 'He was like a magician to me. I think he was one. He could move me as a loadstone moves a speck of steel . . . Yet no,' she added, hearing the infant cry, 'he would not move me now. It would be so unfair to baby.'

'Well,' said Jim, with no great concern (for 'la jalousie rétrospective,' as George Sand calls it, had nearly died out of him),

'however he might move' ee, my love, he'll never come. He swore it to me: and he was a man of his word.'
Midsummer, 1883.

THE END

Freeriver is a community project working to create a place for people to visit and potentially live, long-term, in peace, free from the normal stresses of modern life.

We aim to provide a place where people can spend time discovering themselves and discovering nature. We aim to focus on creativity, health and wellbeing. We plan to provide events and classes for people in the local area and enhance the community.

Please visit our website for more details

www.freerivercommunity.com
freerivercommunity@hotmail.com

www.freerivercommunity.com

Thomas Hardy, (2 June 1840 – 11 January 1928)

Printed in Great Britain
by Amazon

54231163R00046